"He's here?"

Adam turned toward the doorway, wondering if his son could be just a few steps away. Sweat broke out on his forehead at the prospect.

"Was. He left," Nicole said.

Adam didn't know what to feel at this point. He still had so many questions for Nicole, but this twist added another layer. Another obstacle.

Another delay at possibly meeting his son.

"He wasn't supposed to find out like this." Her hand brushed the top of the book. "When I came in, he was just sitting here, bewildered. Confused. And that's how he walked out of here."

"He thinks I abandoned him."

"I'll make him see. It was too much for today."

Adam thought back to Rebecca. He'd believed they'd had a good marriage.

He'd also thought Nicole had left and never came back because she liked the big city over their small town.

Obviously his thoughts weren't to be trusted.

And neither was Nicole.

Lindi Peterson loves writing and reading contemporary Christian romance. She makes her home in northwest Georgia at the foot of the Blue Ridge Mountains with her husband, three cats and one noisy blue-and-gold macaw. She loves to hang out with family and friends, listen to music, and spend time at the beach or the mountains. A member of the Georgia Romance Writers and the Faith, Hope, & Love Christian Writers, she enjoys connecting with readers. You can find her at lindipeterson.com. Fall in love—she dares you!

Books by Lindi Peterson

Love Inspired

Their Surprise Second Chance

Visit the Author Profile page at LoveInspired.com.

Their Surprise
Second Chance

Lindi Peterson

LOVE INSPIRED
INSPIRATIONAL ROMANCE

LOVE INSPIRED®

INSPIRATIONAL ROMANCE

ISBN-13: 978-1-335-59695-6

Their Surprise Second Chance

Copyright © 2023 by Belinda Peterson

For questions and comments about the quality of this book, please contact us at CustomerService@Harlequin.com.

Love Inspired
22 Adelaide St. West, 41st Floor
Toronto, Ontario M5H 4E3, Canada
www.LoveInspired.com

Printed in U.S.A.

O Lord, thou hast searched me, and known me.
—*Psalms* 139:1

To my very own romance hero, Lenny.
Thank you for loving me.

Chapter One

The yellow Victorian with the wraparound porch unexpectedly took Nicole St. John's breath away. Serene, proud, grounded. Everything Nicole wasn't at the moment. Her bright lights, big city attitude that she drove from Chicago to Tennessee with crumbled at the sight of her childhood home.

And she hadn't even stepped inside yet.

She had turned the home over to a rental management company after her father's death, but now that her longtime renters had moved out, Nicole had decided to sell. After having made a life in Lincoln Park, Illinois, with her son, Gavin, over the past twenty-four years, she knew a life back here in Hawks Valley would never be in their future. Selling the house would seal any promise of ever making this town her home again. There were too many painful memories here and, unfortunately, more to make before she said good-bye for good.

Nicole left her suitcases in the trunk as she walked the flat stone path toward the front door, raising her face to the June sunshine glimmering down through the trees. She kicked off her sandals and stood in the grass, wiggling her toes between the green blades—a pleasure the concrete sidewalks of Lincoln Park couldn't give her. Gavin never had the boyhood fun of running in his own yard. Between the parks scattered around the city and his school, she didn't feel her son missed much, although standing in the lush green grass made her wonder. She turned her head as a couple of cars drove slowly down the street. Did the Hendersons or the Millers still live on Valley Way? She hadn't seen anyone from this town since her father's funeral twenty years ago, and even then she hadn't encountered the one person she needed to.

But that person was the one she would finally see while she was here.

With the cars no longer capturing her attention, she started to turn around but abruptly stopped as an older, yet familiar, red pickup came into view, then slowed in front of her house. From where she stood, she couldn't clearly see the face of the driver, but she saw a dark head of hair.

Nicole's heart raced, disbelief shooting through her. There was no way Rowdy Red would still be in commission and Adam Hawk would still be driving that truck twenty-five years later.

Was there?

Not willing to take that chance, she picked up her sandals and quickly made her way up the porch steps. Her mind was scrambled as she shut the front door and leaned against the solid wood—a barrier between her past and her future—hoping if it was Adam, that he hadn't recognized her. Although she had to see him, she also needed a couple of days to settle in. To prepare her heart to tell her son about his father.

A father who didn't know he had a son.

Sweat broke out on her forehead at the mission in front of her, while fear broke out in her heart at what she could lose. But ultimately, love won out over it all and Nicole loved her son enough to admit she couldn't fix his situation.

And the only person who could didn't know he existed.

She glanced up at the foyer's chandelier hanging overhead, as its sparkling crystals twinkled in the sunlight. She counted to ten twice, finally letting out a breath convinced that the truck hadn't stopped. Her breathing started to return to normal and she set her sandals down, feeling ridiculously like a teenager even though she just turned forty-three. Taking a few steps forward, she allowed her gaze to scan the living room, the cream-colored curtains framing an otherwise empty space. She paused in the sunroom, pushing thoughts of Adam and her mission away, and breathed in the memories the red and yellow custom decor evoked. The couch she and her friends sat on drinking lemonade, eating homemade cookies and talking about boys.

Although she never talked about Adam. He'd been her secret crush.

Moving into the kitchen, she allowed the vintage quaintness of the room to bring forth images of family dinners and conversation. Unable to resist, she stepped over to the bay window, pulled back the yellow gingham curtain and smiled at the penciled "NICOLE + ADAM" that she'd written down the side of the wall by the window frame. She'd written her name when she was a child. She'd added Adam's name as a teen, its cursive bent a giveaway at the time lapse. Either no one had noticed or no one cared to remove it. The penciled scripts, now faint to be sure, took her back years. She promised herself she would erase both names before she left. Nicole plus Adam hadn't worked out back then.

And they certainly weren't going to work out now.

She would add the task to the to-do list tucked inside her purse. Gavin would be here in a week and unbeknownst to him, he would meet his father. Fear, wonder and regret tumbled through her all at once. Her uncomplicated, quiet life would soon be no more. She'd be fielding questions and probably facing disbelief. Everything she had to say was the truth. A truth that she should have revealed years ago.

A whoosh she didn't expect washed over her. These feelings of nostalgia and regret couldn't keep happening. They were dangerous. Threatening. Just like possibly seeing Adam outside her home.

Which was better than seeing him inside her home.

But that was exactly what happened when she turned away from the hidden, unfulfilled, childish dreams penciled down the wall. He stood in the doorway of her kitchen, the brightly lit foyer causing his face to be shadowed, but unlike the uncertainty when she couldn't clearly see who drove the truck, there was no denying who stood in her house now.

Adam Hawk.

"IIi, Nicole. It is you." Adam's memories instantly tumbled back through childhood, adolescence, then high school. He and Nicole had maneuvered the Hawks Valley school system together from kindergarten through graduation. He swallowed hard, remembering the short time they dated while he and Rebecca were broken up. Regret and awkwardness filled him unexpectedly, making him question why he really did pull into her driveway when he thought he saw her standing in front of the house.

"It's me. Did you knock, and I didn't hear you? Or do you always just walk into people's houses uninvited?"

Uninvited. That word couldn't be misconstrued. He half turned, pointing to the door. "I saw you in the front yard. Well, at least I thought it was you. Then the door was open slightly, so I stepped in." Could he bumble this conversation any more? He hadn't expected the dark-haired beauty to captivate him after all these years. Her deep brown eyes seemed more soulful, her dark brown hair still long, with a touch of gray here and there being the only giveaway that time had passed.

"The door was open?" Nicole stepped around him into the foyer, to push the big wooden door shut. As she let go, it slowly started moving inward.

"Looks like the knob might need to be replaced." He walked over and jiggled the knob, turning it to the left. He then pushed the door and it stayed shut. "Yep. Just make sure you give it a good twist to the left as you close it." How mundane and normal this conversation sounded in this totally abnormal situation.

"Thank you. I'll see about having it fixed or replaced." She opened the door and stepped onto the porch and he followed. It was her polite way of bringing life to that "uninvited" word, he surmised. Could he blame her? He ran his hand through his hair, wondering how much, if anything, she held against him for his behavior all those years ago.

"Are you moving back?" He had to ask. Had to know.

"No. I'm actually here to sell the house."

Her unexpected words punched his gut. *Sell?* The Victorian had been in the St. John family for generations. "I'm surprised. I thought with you renting it out for so long, you might move back someday."

Her gaze, never landing on his for long, scanned the yard. "No. I have a great life in Lincoln Park. Good job, good friends. It's time to sell."

He couldn't tell for sure without awkwardly staring, but he thought there were tears in her eyes. Her voice had caught when she said the word "sell." Were there money problems that were forcing her to put the house on the market? "If there's anything I can do while you're here, let me know. How long are you staying?"

"A couple of weeks. And, Adam, I do need to talk to you about something…"

His radar sounded. So her strange behavior hadn't been imagined after all. "Sure. I've got a few minutes. My mom dropped Kylie, my daughter, off at dance class but I need to pick her up. I'm sure you heard about Rebecca's passing." There was still such a mix of emotions when he thought about his wife. The woman he thought he knew but apparently hadn't.

Nicole looked down, her toe trying to dig a hole through the wooden board. "Yes, I heard. I'm sorry for your loss. And actually, our conversation might take longer than a few minutes. Maybe we can set up a time in the next couple of days? I'll be here cleaning out the garage."

The almost robotic sound of her voice curled his insides, giving her untold revelation weight. If his mom didn't have a hair appointment, he'd call her to pick up Kylie. But that wasn't an option. "Sure. Why don't I stop back by tomorrow? Maybe after lunch?"

Nicole nodded. "That sounds good. I'll be here. See you then." She pointed to the driveway. "You still have that truck?"

"Oh, yes. I'm not parting with Rowdy anytime soon. That truck has been an important part of my life since, well, you know, my dad gave it to me. I was sixteen."

She hung her head for a moment. "I remember. See you tomorrow."

He thought her eyes were a little misty, but she retreated into her house before he could say anything, even good-bye. Shoving his hands in his pockets, he jaunted down the stairs, his mind in a whirlwind. Her seriousness had him puzzled. And her reminders of the past... Well, they left him concerned. He hadn't thought about his dad giving him that truck in a while.

And her asking to talk to him had him more than a little nervous.

Scenarios of what she could want to speak to him about raced through his mind as he drove to the dance studio, but they all reached dead ends. He remembered wondering about her over the years. Those months after high school graduation were fuzzy, even back then. His upcoming wedding, his father's passing, blurred the summer months, making them hard to recall. Duty guided him to make the moves necessary to live. He did remember thinking he had made the right decision in taking Rebecca back, even though he had started to have feelings for Nicole, when he realized his childhood friend had bolted from town right after graduation. No one heard from her, and it was as if she vanished. Then, when her father passed away, he had been at special pilots' training the week the funeral was held. She'd already been gone by the time he returned.

In the early years of marriage, Rebecca's miscarriage and infertility issues had him wondering what a normal marriage looked like, because his didn't seem to be one. He knew marriage was hard work, but it shouldn't feel like a chore. Sure, they had some good times, but the weight of not having children led them down to places he never knew existed. Then, when she did become pregnant, their troubles ended.

Or so he thought.

Kylie immediately became his joy and heart. He and

Rebecca had settled into a nice routine. Again, his perception, apparently. Then, a little over two years ago, when the sheriff came to the door after the single car accident, Adam's world crumbled. Fear of raising a daughter alone consumed his mind, and the adjustment to everyday life without Rebecca took time.

His mom helped hold them all together. She watched Kylie when he worked. Flying became his only safe place. A place where he could rise above everything, literally, and gain new perspective. His job had been a therapy all its own, and he thanked God for it every day.

Loud music greeted him at the Woodvale Dance Studio as he arrived a couple of minutes early. The students were following the instructor's lead, most of them on point. Kylie, he noticed, always stayed one or two beats behind, but his six-year-old had such a passion for dancing. He had arranged private lessons for Kylie, which she would start soon.

The music stopped and the teacher, Lark Woodvale, gave the students a round of applause before reminding them to practice at home. After gathering her backpack, Kylie ran over to him and hugged him around the legs. "Hi, Daddy! Did you watch me? Was I good?"

Adam rubbed the top of her head. "You were great."

"Hi, Adam." Lark walked over, wiping her forehead with a towel, her long blond hair secured in a bun.

"Hey. Great job. The kids seem to love this class. And it's good exercise."

She nodded. "It's fun, too, I hope."

"I'll be right back, Daddy." Kylie ran with a few other girls toward the restroom.

"So…" Lark crossed her arms, studying him closely. "Did you hear Nicole St. John is in town? Selling the

Victorian? I never thought she'd sell the house after all these years."

News traveled that fast? "How did you know? She just arrived this afternoon."

"You know this town. Buzzing already. I mean, she hasn't been here in years, and now, she swoops in to sell one of the most beautiful historic homes in town like it's nothing."

Adam realized all the assumptions in the woman's diatribe. While true he hadn't talked to Nicole all that long, assuming there wasn't any emotion in her decision seemed like a stretch to Adam. "I'm sure she has good reasons for her decision."

Lark nodded. "Maybe. Hey, didn't you two date in high school? Or go to the prom or something? I know I was a couple of years behind you guys, but our cheer squad always knew the scoop."

All those memories rushed through Adam again. The regretful prom night with Nicole that had brought out hidden feelings for his high school best friend. Those feelings led to him proposing to Rebecca out of guilt two weeks later. Nicole must not have been that affected because she left for college in the Chicago area right after graduation, and except for her father's funeral, hadn't been back. "We went to prom and had a couple of dates. Nothing serious. Nicole and I have always been good friends."

Thankfully Kylie chose that moment to return. "Grab your backpack, princess. We need to go. See you next week, Lark."

"See you. Kylie, don't forget to practice those moves. You're doing great."

As his daughter settled into her seat, Adam started his truck. The roar of the engine reminded him of the here and now. The present. The life he'd built with Kylie in this town, Hawks Valley, named after his ancestors.

This reminder served him well. He needed to stay in the present and stop drifting to the past. Nicole's return would be brief. And except for a conversation they would have tomorrow, her return would have no effect on his life.

Putting his truck into reverse, his thoughts once again drifted back all those years. But only for a moment. Shoving the gear shift into drive, he moved forward, pushing the upcoming conversation with Nicole out of his mind.

Except her words kept replaying. The one word that stuck in his mind was "need." What could she *need* to talk to him about? He sighed. No point in stressing over it. This time tomorrow, he would know and would probably be laughing at how he'd built up her words when they were really nothing.

At least he hoped so.

Chapter Two

Nicole flipped open the book.

The book.

The picture of Gavin taken at the hospital twenty-four-years ago stared up at her, as did her own handwritten words stating the date, time, height and weight of her baby boy. Below the mandatory statistics, she had written a short paragraph.

Adam. How I wish you were here. Your baby boy is beautiful. He looks just like you. Your nose and mouth. His deep blue eyes mirror yours. The nurses told me they might change color. I assured them they wouldn't. I'm confident he'll have the same beautiful eyes you do. I wish everything could be different. Not with Gavin. I love him so much already. But with you. Maybe someday...

Nicole flipped page after page, each one highlighting Gavin's life as he grew. Each note still wishful, yet becoming more doubtful. As Gavin grew and they became established in their community, Nicole watched her son become a responsible, respectful young man.

Closing the book with more force than necessary, Nicole tried to figure out why she suddenly felt trapped. Trapped to tell Adam, which sounded ridiculous because no one knew and the decision to tell him had been made by her alone. No words had been spoken yet, except for her telling her childhood friend she needed to talk to him, and she could make up anything vague at this point.

But she opened the book again to the first page and wondered. What would Adam say? Would he hate her? Would the book prove anything? What if he didn't want to meet Gavin? Adam did have a six-year-old daughter he was raising.

The doorbell rang, startling her. She quickly hid the book in the storage below the bay window seat before making her way to the door. At least she had mastered the hang of making sure it stayed closed. She opened the door to find Adam, his mother Shelley, and a small girl who must be his daughter. Even at such a young age, she looked like Rebecca, but with Adam's dark hair and blue eyes. "Hello."

"Nicole St. John. You're as beautiful as you were cheering on that field in high school." Adam's mom pulled her into a hug, taking Nicole by surprise.

"Why, thank you. I hardly remember those days—it's been so long. Please come in." She stepped back, holding the door as Adam and his family passed by, a blur of what Nicole had envisioned for her life for so many years. Shelley, still stylish, had aged gracefully and beautifully, her smile still lighting up everyone around her.

"Nicole," Adam said, "this is my daughter Kylie. Kylie, this is Ms. St. John. We grew up and went to school together."

"Hi, Ms. St. John." Kylie stayed close to her dad. Her

dark hair had been pulled into pigtails with bright blue ribbons, which highlighted those Hawk family eyes.

Those bluer than blue eyes. Like Gavin.

Oh, my.

"You can call me Nicole. It's nice to meet you." Her words came out automatically because she wasn't sure it was nice at all. Meeting Kylie made everything more complicated, although if Gavin stayed in Adam's life, Kylie would be a part of that. And since Nicole was Gavin's mom, this weaved a tapestry filled with flaws.

Nicole found herself looking too far ahead. Way too far.

"It's going to be odd seeing a realtor sign in your front yard, Nicole," Shelley said. "Not many homes go up for sale around here. The Victorian is still beautiful, though. I see a touch of your mom here and there."

Nicole had purposefully ignored anything personal except for her own pencil art on the wall in the seating area. If she thought too much about the memories, she might become too sentimental and that wouldn't be good.

"I know. I'm hoping it will sell fast."

Shelley held out a bag she'd been carrying. "I hope you don't mind us barging in like this. When Adam told me he talked to you, I just knew we had to bring you dinner, what with you traveling most of the day. It's not much, mind you. Just my chicken salad and bread and butter pickles. And Kylie and I baked you a lemon pound cake. I remembered it was your favorite."

Church picnics and yearly festivals played through Nicole's mind. Funerals, too. Shelley Hawk's lemon pound cake was a staple at the happy and sad occasions one found themselves at in Hawks Valley. "Thank you. This is unnecessary but appreciated." Nicole headed for the kitchen where she set the bag on the counter.

Gavin loved chicken salad.

She looked at the bay window, where *the* book hid beneath the wooden bench. One small book, one big predicament, all tucked under brightly colored floral cushions.

"I like this kitchen, Daddy. It's bright and sunny, like ours." Kylie stood looking out the window, inches from *the* book that revealed the life of her half brother.

Nicole crossed her arms, taking a deep breath. Sweat broke out on her forehead. These people standing in her kitchen would forever be in her life when she disclosed her quarter-century-old secret.

And Adam.

Nicole longed to see Adam look at Gavin the way he looked at Kylie. The man obviously doted on his daughter. Would he dote on Gavin, too? Was that even the right word when it came to a father and a grown son?

It fell all over Nicole how she came here wanting a kind of healer for her son, but Adam was so much more. He was his father.

She almost couldn't breathe. How long were they staying?

"This kitchen is just one of the features that will sell this house right away. I always loved this custom table your parents had built to fit perfectly into this bay window area." Shelley ran her fingers over the wooden table as she stood near Adam and Kylie. A close-knit family.

Nicole tried to picture Gavin in the mix. Would he be standing to the left of Adam on the end? Behind his grandma? Next to his sister?

Another cold sweat. She had to stop. No one knew.
Yet.

What would life look like in a week? In a month? Would these welcoming smiles and easy banter still be a part of her life? Or would she be on the outside look-ing in to a life her son had without her?

Adam took the containers out of the bag and put them in the refrigerator. "This visit is actually double duty. We did want to bring you a meal, but I thought this might be a good time to talk about whatever it was you wanted to discuss."

She quickly glanced between Adam and his mom and daughter. There was no way she could have the conver-sation with Shelley and Kylie here. She took a gulp of water from her cup on the counter, her dry mouth beg-ging for relief. Gavin mimicked Adam in so many ways and mannerisms. Watching Adam mirrored watching an older version of her son.

Almost like she could see into the future.

But her future was anything but certain.

This man had the power to ruin her life. And he didn't even know it.

"I'm not sure this is the time for our conversation." She kept her voice low while nodding toward Shelley and Kylie who had turned to look out the window, a cardinal bath-ing in the birdbath capturing their attention.

His deep blue eyes acknowledged her nod. He held on to the counter with one hand, like he needed steadying. Like he knew the seriousness of the conversation. "Mom. Why don't you take Kylie to the park? Nicole and I have a couple of things to talk about. There's no sense in you and Kylie hanging inside on such a nice day."

Kylie jumped up and down. "Yay, Grandma! Can we go to the park?"

Shelley shifted her gaze between Adam and Nicole, her smile placing the wrong tone on the upcoming con-versation. His mom had always been a fan of hers and had taken so many pictures prom night, like she knew it would be the only time they'd have a real date. And she'd been right. Two weeks later, Adam had been back with Rebecca.

Shelley grabbed Kylie's hand. "Yes. Let's go to the park. We can walk from here. Adam, just drive down and pick us up when you are done." The older woman turned toward her. "And Nicole...we're so glad you're back in town. Maybe you'll change your mind about selling and stay here in Hawks Valley."

Nicole smiled but didn't respond. Adam gave his mom and Kylie a hug with the promise he'd be down to pick them up soon.

Pressure, a hundred times worse than she imagined, coursed through her. *Oh, hi, you have a twenty-four-year-old son who needs you. Now go pick up your mom and daughter.*

But what choice did she have?

Adam stood on Nicole's front porch, watching his mom and Kylie walk hand in hand toward the park. He delayed going back in. The air had shifted inside when Nicole nodded toward his mom. He knew then that the information Nicole wanted to share with him wasn't casual. His gut and his head knew it.

He'd been in a few precarious situations as a pilot where he had to act fast and make decisions based on instinct. Following his mom and Kylie seemed the safest escape right now, but he stood his ground on the porch. He took a couple of deep breaths before heading back into the Victorian. His footsteps echoed through the house as he made his way to the kitchen where he left Nicole.

Had he given her time to regroup? Thinking back, he remembered that her body language had screamed tension ever since they arrived. Her smile never fully evolved and her gaze darted between them all, probably looking for a safe place to land.

When he entered the kitchen, she sat at the table, her hands on a book. He slowed his steps as he realized the book resembled a scrapbook or photo album. The chair scraped as he pulled it out—a hint of foreboding, he surmised.

Sitting this close to Nicole, her natural beauty struck him. No makeup that he could see. Just her deep brown eyes beckoning him.

He had become lost in those eyes the spring of their senior year, which led to a night that shouldn't have happened. His gaze shifted to the photo album held tightly in her hands, with a baby photo on the front.

His heart stopped momentarily.

He knew.

Swallowing hard, heart about to thump out of his chest, he couldn't speak. He could only wait until her grasp loosened on the album. The album he knew would change his life forever.

"Adam."

"Nicole." His gaze shifted downward, his index finger touching the album. "Show me."

"Adam, I…" Tears pooled in her eyes.

"I want to see my child." He barely squeezed out the words. They sounded choppy and uncertain, but he wasn't wrong. He knew it.

She slowly opened the leather-bound album and wiped a tear off the first page as she turned the book toward him. "His name is Gavin."

Gavin. "Gavin. Okay." Shock, disbelief and every other emotion possible held his gaze to the page. He saw words written on the page below the hospital photo, but they blurred at the sight of his son. Adam touched the photo like he could bring it to life. The baby, Gavin, reminded him of Kylie at birth. The same dark hair, eyes, nose.

He sucked in a breath. Kylie had a brother. A big brother.

Adam stood, forcing his gaze away from the photo. "I don't understand. Why didn't you tell me?"

Her fingers dabbed at the corners of her eyes. "I wanted to. I came back the week of the Fourth of July to tell you, but your dad had just died, and when I saw yours and Rebecca's wedding invitation on my dad's table, I freaked. I ran. I thought I had time. I wanted to tell you when I came back a few years later for my father's funeral, but you weren't here."

"Your father died twenty years ago." He picked up the photo album, his mind whirling with reasons why she never told him. The reasons faded as he unfolded Gavin's life, page by page. His son.

His *son.*

Would he ever become used to saying those words?

He doubted he would.

The resemblance to himself, physically and career-wise, kept him flipping pages back and forth. "This is incredible. You've kept track of everything. I have so many questions. I don't know where to begin…"

"He needs you."

Her words gutted him. "What's wrong?"

"He's a pilot, Adam. And he was involved in a plane crash."

Adam grabbed the back of the chair with his free hand, memories of his father flooding him. "He survived?"

"Physically? Yes. Mentally, he's not the same. He won't fly. It's funny. I tried for so many years to steer him away from everything aviation-related. Now I'd do anything to have him return to flying. I'm even doing the thing I never thought I'd do."

She quickly looked down as if she didn't mean to say those words out loud. But she had.

His phone dinged. Hands shaking, he set the book on the table, then pulled his phone out of his pocket. "Kylie got stung by a bee and they're on their way back from the park." He shook his head. "I have to process this before telling them. Can I come back later tonight? I'm sure my mom will watch Kylie." Nicole had to say yes. He had too many questions to wait until tomorrow.

"Sure."

Anger? Joy? Unsure of which emotion gripped him more, he tried to settle his mind.

Part of him wanted to pull every bit of information about Gavin out of her while another part wanted to hug her at this revelation. He wanted to place his hands on each side of her face to see into her mind, to grasp everything he'd missed regarding Gavin. He clenched his hands to his sides, knowing all of this would have to wait.

The kitchen faded as he walked to the front door, unable to say anything else to Nicole. He made his way down the steps, his mind barely in the present. He steadied his shaking hands by pulling his keys out of his pocket. His mom and Kylie approached, unaware their lives were forever changed. A son. Gavin.

The thought wouldn't leave his mind. For the next few hours he had to pretend like his world hadn't been rocked. Again. By another woman. Couldn't they tell the truth?

Sucking in a much-needed breath, he knew he couldn't compare the two women. They were very different. Even after he learned that Rebecca had been on her way home from a divorce attorney when she wrecked the car, he still struggled with her death.

With unanswered questions.

Never mind Kylie who had just recently found her new sense of normal. And now he would have to tell her she had a brother. A big brother.

He turned the ignition on, setting the air on high.

"Daddy!"

He jumped out in time to pick Kylie off the ground and give her a big hug. Overcompensating, he knew. "Are you okay?"

"Daddy, you're squeezing my stung arm."

He loosened his grip, wishing he never had to put her down. Her dark curls and blue eyes were his happiness. He would never willingly do anything to hurt her. But how would she react to this news?

"Does it hurt badly?" he asked.

"She'll be okay. Just need to put some ice on it." His mom looked at him questioningly as she buckled up. "Did you and Nicole catch up? What has she been doing all these years?"

He made more work out of helping Kylie buckle up than needed, but it gave him a few moments. Luckily his mom's questions all ran together and she probably didn't expect all the answers. *She's good. She's been raising our son the last twenty-four years.*

He cocked the air vent right on his face and blew out a breath before backing down the driveway. "She's good."

One of Kylie's favorite country songs came on the radio. Adam turned up the volume, thanking God for that intervention while praying for more as the afternoon turned into evening. He knew it would be the only way he'd make it until he returned to Nicole's house to learn more about his son.

Chapter Three

Nicole wiped her eyes, dried her tears, then washed her face. She couldn't sit here in the house waiting on Adam's return. She needed a change of scenery. Already the kitchen had turned into a place for lost appetites and tears.

She pulled the door shut with that purposeful twist to the left. No one locked their doors in Hawks Valley, but she could make sure it shut tight. What a refreshing difference from city life. A quick walk to the downtown area revived her. While a lot of things had changed, a few were the same. HV Hardware, the Hawks Valley Theatre, Turn the Page book shop, and The Corner Diner all reminded her of high school days and nights hanging with friends.

But it was the old coffee shop that had been totally renovated and renamed The Morning Grind that beckoned her inside. Fresh, clean paint and decor reminded her of her favorite coffee shop in Lincoln Park. Americana music played softly overhead, creating a workable ambiance. Conversation could be held without yelling and the sweet, enticing smell had her wanting to try everything on the menu.

She ordered her standard almond milk latte, added a blueberry muffin and gave the barista her first name.

"Hi, Nicole. Are you new here? I don't remember seeing you before." The brown-haired woman grabbed a cup and wrote Nicole's name on it. She had a pretty face, and for some reason she looked familiar.

But Nicole knew that wasn't possible. She had been gone too long. "I grew up in Hawks Valley. I'm just back to sell my house I've been renting out."

"Welcome back. At least for a while, I guess. I'm Rachel. The owner."

"Hi, Rachel. I'm Nicole. The drifter." They both smiled at Nicole's attempt at a joke.

"It's good to meet you. I hope you come back while you're here."

"This place smells incredible. I'm sure I'll be back."

After receiving her drink and muffin, Nicole settled into a corner table for two, replaying this afternoon in her mind. The coffee tasted amazing, as did the muffin, but everything paled in comparison to her conversation with Adam. She looked at her phone, Gavin's smiling face making the whole world better again. Made every tear worth crying.

At least for a moment.

"I'm doing this for you. I promise." She whispered the words, but they were loud in her heart.

Not knowing what time Adam would be arriving, she decided she'd better not stay gone too long. She threw her muffin wrapper in the trash and grabbed her coffee.

"Bye, Nicole. See you soon."

Nicole smiled at the warm good-bye. "Yes. Everything tasted great by the way. Loved it."

Rachel nodded. "Thanks."

She sipped her coffee while she walked back to her

house. The Victorian still belonged to her until it sold. There were two storage areas in the garage that housed the push mower and gardening tools, but Nicole knew all that had to go when she put the house on the market. That task would help keep her mind busy until next week when Gavin would be here.

Gavin. Here. In Hawks Valley.

Meeting Adam…his father.

Adam didn't appear to hate her. Although he was still in shock, she assumed. Tonight would tell a better tale about his true feelings. She didn't expect to escape an array of emotions, including anger. He seemed enthralled with the book, though. He'd read every page, some more than once.

Nicole knew she needed to mentally prepare for tonight. All the questions. She didn't know if she would have all the answers. And hoped she didn't have to mumble out a lot of "I don't knows."

The sunshine bathed her arms as she walked. Nicole sighed as the trees rustled softly in the breeze, the scent of the river reminding her of childhood summer days. She passed the Harrisons' house, the American flag still flying from the right side of the garage.

"Ouch." She stubbed her toe slightly on a cracked sidewalk. No blood. All good. She licked coffee that had splashed on the lid. The proud, stately Victorian came into view. Taking another sip of her coffee, she half choked at the sight in the driveway.

Gavin's car.

Her feet froze on the sidewalk, refusing to take another step. Why was he here a week early?

The book.

Blood drained every which way through her body as visions of the book sitting on the breakfast table looped through her mind. She had to push herself to move as her fear would leave her stranded on the sidewalk.

Nicole had no idea how she made it in the house, but she did. And she didn't have to wonder where she'd find Gavin. Tears streamed down her face as she found him right where she knew she would. He sat at the table, his tall frame bent over the book.

He looked up, his face unreadable.

"Gavin," she stammered, attempting a smile but failing miserably.

"Ma. What is this? Who's Adam?"

Timidly, she walked toward him, setting her coffee on the counter. "Gavin. I—"

"Adam is my dad, isn't he? And he lives here, in Hawks Valley."

"Yes." She had no idea how she pushed that word out of her tight throat.

Gavin shut the book. "And he's a pilot. Like me. Or me, like him." He stood, his words monotone, like his life lately. Emotionless and flat. Surely he felt something right now?

"I didn't want you to find out this way. I was going to tell you when you got here. But you came early."

"I guess I ruined all your plans." He nodded at the book. "Again."

Her mind whirled. "No. You didn't. You've never ruined anything. You've only made things better."

He shoved his hands in his pockets, his face unreadable. "All these years and you've never said a word. Just kept a creepy scrapbook like you could sum up my life with a few pictures and words to a man who never wanted to know me. Do you have another hidden book about him that you need to show me?"

His words took her breath away. She bit back a retort

that would make this about her and tried to see inside *his* head. *His* feelings. "Gavin…this is complicated. I made what I thought was the best decision at the time. Maybe it was, maybe it wasn't. I was only looking out for you and what would be best for you."

"Yeah, like keeping a kid's dad from him was the best."

He wouldn't even look at her, breaking her mom heart into tiny shreds. "I can't change the past. But Adam is coming here in a little while. You'll be able to meet him."

Gavin pulled his hands out of his pockets, one of them holding a set of keys. "I don't want to meet him. Not today. Not ever."

Those words she didn't expect. "Not today then. I'll call him and tell him not to come."

"I feel like I don't know you, Ma. It was just me and you all these years, but my dad was living here, eight hours away. I don't understand. Who are you? Are you really my Ma? I feel like my whole life has been a sham. Like a bad movie."

Nicole stepped toward him, and he backed up. "Gavin. Of course I'm your mom. Let's sit. I can try to explain…"

His blue eyes stared blankly at the ceiling. He needed a haircut, but she always loved the rumpled look of her son. He was tall and lean. Wise and compassionate. She wouldn't change a thing about him. Pulling out a chair, she moved to sit, hopeful he would follow suit.

Instead, he picked up his phone off the table, glancing at the screen. "I know I said I'd help you, Ma, but I can't stay here knowing the man who didn't want anything to do with me lives so close."

She took a deep breath. "He didn't know about you." *There. I said the words.* The words that could change her son's opinion about her forever.

Gavin shook his head full of hair. "Nice try. Don't take the blame for him."

Her already shattered heart sunk at the mess she'd made. "I'm not. He didn't know until a few hours ago."

A fake half smile graced his face. "Maybe that's true, maybe not. I don't know anything anymore. What kind of guy doesn't check on a girl… Look, I can't stay here. I'll call you soon, but I gotta go."

The chair scraped the wood floor as she stood. "Please stay. We can talk this out. I can explain everything."

He walked toward her, giving her hope. Taking her hands in his, he squeezed them, his keychain dangling from his pinky. "Ma. You can't fix everything all the time. I'll call you."

His touch left her, then he walked out of the kitchen.

"I love you." She could barely croak out the words through her tears.

Footsteps stopped, but he didn't turn around. "Love you."

Nicole wanted to run after her son, but her feet stayed rooted to the floor. Besides, what could she say at this point that wouldn't make the situation worse? He already had the wrong idea about the situation. Her attempts to change his mind right now would only reinforce what she believed was the truth.

Which wasn't the truth at all.

But who was she to talk about truth?

She'd lived a lie the last twenty-five years of her life.

"I think there's still something you're not telling me."

Adam shifted his gaze away from his mom. He wasn't in the habit of keeping things from her. The need to know more about Gavin drove his commitment to not say anything to anyone until he talked to Nicole again. He still had no idea how he would explain all this to his daughter. Her pureness and innocence kept him from wanting to tell her at all.

"Mom. It's all good. I'm just going to talk to Nicole. It might get late. We have a lot of catching up to do."

"You don't fool me, Adam Hawk. But go and make goo-goo eyes at her. I thought you two belonged together when you dated as teens. Not that I didn't love Rebecca. I did. And Kylie is my life. In fact, let her spend the night. Have a good time. I'll see you tomorrow when you get off work at the airport."

Adam drove in silence to Nicole's, then quickly parked and got out, his indignation causing him to take the porch steps two at a time. He hoped Nicole was ready with answers. The door opened before Adam could even knock. A teary-eyed but still beautiful Nicole ushered him inside to the kitchen. The book lay open—no doubt the cause of her distress.

Her eyes were different, though. More soulful, despondent. The rebuttal he rehearsed all afternoon stayed locked in his mind, refusing to surface into words of accusation.

"Gavin was here."

He took a deep breath. "He's here?" He turned toward the doorway, wondering if his son could be just a few steps away. Sweat broke out on his forehead at the prospect.

"Was. He left."

"I don't understand."

He listened while Nicole briefed him on the conversation between her and Gavin. Her nervous sounding voice betrayed the depth of her hurt. Her son—*their* son—had left, confused and possibly misled if he didn't believe Nicole's words about Adam just finding out he existed.

Adam didn't know what to feel at this point. He still had so many questions for Nicole, but this twist added another layer. Another obstacle.

Another delay at possibly meeting his son.

Lord, help me.

"He was already wounded, Adam. He wasn't supposed to find out like this." Her hand brushed the top of the book. When I came in, he was just sitting here, bewildered. Confused. And that's how he walked out of here."

"He thinks I abandoned him."

"I tried to explain but he wasn't hearing what I was trying to tell him. I'll make him see. It was just too much for today."

Adam thought back to Rebecca. It wasn't until two days after she died that he found out she had been driving from an attorney's office where she had started divorce proceedings when she wrecked the car. He thought they'd had a good marriage.

He also thought Nicole left and never came back because she liked the big city over their small town.

Obviously his thoughts weren't to be trusted.

And neither was Nicole. She'd blindsided him with this news, just like the lawyer had blindsided him about Rebecca. Both women, by omission, had lied to him for years.

Could he even trust Nicole again?

Adam pulled out a chair and sat across from the mother of his son. Nicole's hands wrapped around a mug with the silhouette of the mountains and river peeking through her fingers. He noticed then she wasn't wearing any rings. "You're not married?"

She shook her head. "No. It's just been me and Gavin all these years."

Adam's mind swirled with the weight of it all. The two

of them navigating life on their own. "I saw the book, the notes, but tell me more about Gavin. Tell me everything."

"Like I said before, I came back to tell you about him. But with your father's crash and your upcoming wedding, I fled, fast. Then I kept putting off telling you, but Gavin and I were making it. We had a great relationship. He was such a good kid, then grew into a responsible young man."

Nicole spent the next two hours telling him about his son's life: How he snuck behind her back to take flying lessons while he was in college earning a bachelor's in communication. How he graduated from the University of Tennessee last year, then showed Nicole his pilot's license.

"I've never been so proud and scared all in the same day." She looked out the window. "I'd give anything to go back to that day. *Anything.*"

"What would you have done differently?"

"I'd have told him about you. Then I might have shown him the book." She pushed back the chair. "I say all that, but I don't know. I didn't want to tell him about you until I knew how you would react. I thought my worst fear was his flying and crashing. Now I know my worst fear was you rejecting him."

"But I didn't."

"He thinks you did. And that's my fault," she admitted.

Nicole pulled a sweater off the chair and walked outside. He followed, not sure what to say. Yes, it was her fault, but not on purpose.

Adam took a deep breath. "Where do we go from here?"
"We?"

Nightfall had brought the cool Tennessee air, its gentle beginning-of-summer-breeze lightly lifting strands of Nicole's dark hair. The back porch light cast a long shadow across freshly cut grass. He stood slightly behind her, wanting to offer words of comfort. But they wouldn't come. How easy it would be to wrap her into his arms, but he knew that would complicate everything that wasn't already complicated. They needed some measure of distance. "Yes, we." He'd keep the togetherness on a verbal basis only. "You want your son to know the truth. I want to know my son. How long are you staying?"

She half turned. "A couple of weeks. I'm a teacher, so I have the summer off, but I need to put the house on the market and go back home."

"And me and Gavin? How do we fit into your plan?" He hadn't wanted to sound snarky, but knew his tone betrayed him.

She took a few steps and settled on the wooden swing that hung from a huge oak tree. "Valid question. I wanted to talk to you, then, if you were agreeable, tell Gavin about you. You're both adults. I figured I'd bow out and let you two take it from there."

"That's a tall order, Nicole. I'm a dad of a six-year-old girl. Gavin is a twenty-four-year-old man. Big difference. What made you think I would know what I'm doing? That I would say and do the right things?"

As Nicole pushed with her feet, the swing slowly moved. She still looked like the girl he grew up with. Fun, whimsical, outgoing. Everything Rebecca hadn't been.

"You're Adam. You always said and did the right things." She stopped the swing abruptly. "Tell me about flying. What's the draw? Why has Gavin always been obsessed with becoming a pilot?"

He shoved a hand in his pocket. "Not sure there are enough words to describe it, Nicole. It's exhilarating, fast, breathtaking. There's just something—in the Hawk blood, obviously—that keeps us in the air."

"You know, the name Gavin means white hawk."

His heart skipped and his throat dried. "It does?"

"Yes. I wanted him to have a part of his heritage, even if he never came to know you."

Nicole's actions led to such a mix of emotions. He couldn't change any decisions she'd made in the past, but he could have input into all future decisions regarding their son. "Just like everything else about this situation, I don't know what to say. Thank you seems inadequate."

"I wish I knew where he went, and I wish he hadn't left in such a despondent mood with so many unanswered questions. It's all such a mess. A mess I've made."

"Quit saying 'I.' From this day forward, we're a 'we' when it comes to Gavin and his well-being." Again, the thought overwhelmed him. He had a daughter, a mom and friends he would have to tell that he had a son. His lips threatened to turn upward in a smile. Now that hours had passed, the word "son" had settled into his heart in a way he hadn't thought possible.

"Fine…we. What are *we* going to do?"

"We are going to find Gavin, explain what happened, introduce him to Kylie and my mom. His family." He swallowed hard. The words pushed forth, but putting them into action would be harder. Probably more difficult than anything he'd ever done. He'd thought telling his mom about Rebecca's visit to the divorce attorney had been hard. But that seemed like a day at a picnic compared to this task.

Task.

No, not task. This involved Gavin. His son. A pilot. A look-alike—not only from the pictures in the book, but also from the recent pictures Nicole had shown him.

Would he and Gavin ever take a picture together?

Nicole stood, keeping one hand on the swing rope. "Gavin was supposed to help me clean out the garage. I thought we'd have a couple of days together before he found out about you. Not only am I missing that bonding time with my son, I guess I'm on my own now to purge those old tools."

His first instinct was to offer to help, but he bit his tongue. Becoming involved with Nicole wasn't an option. As vulnerable as things were right now, they had no future together except to guide Gavin in his life choices. Sure, he would see Nicole at family events like weddings and holiday gatherings, but that was as far as they could go.

And right now, he needed to figure out how to tell his mom and Kylie. That he could do on his own, but he wouldn't leave Nicole alone to find Gavin. He couldn't.

He wanted to find his son and get to know him. "I'm sure Gavin won't stay gone long. Like you said, he was shocked and confused. Give him a couple of days."

"I'll go with you to tell your mom." Even in the dark of the night, he could see her gaze looking at him through lowered lids. Like her offer was sincere and scary.

Her gesture surprised, yet settled him. "I'd like that."

She needed him. He probably needed her. Needs and wants were different. As long as they stayed on a need level he could deal.

But never again would he be on a want basis with Nicole St. John.

Chapter Four

Nicole needed a break. And she needed help.

She had started cleaning out the storage units in the garage, having no idea how many screws, nuts, bolts and other assorted items her father had left. She needed Gavin.

Pulling her hair into a ponytail, she tried not to dwell on the unreturned texts and phone calls. It had only been a day. A very long day. One sleep, as she used to tell him when he was little.

How many more sleeps would she have before she heard from her son?

She used her favorite facial cleanser and wiped the grime from being in the hot garage off her face. Feeling refreshed, she grabbed her purse and headed to the coffee shop. Maybe Rachel would be there. She seemed friendly and nice, and Nicole needed nice right now.

It would be refreshing to have another female to chat with about fashion, books, anything other than real life. Nicole missed her friends from home, but it was that time of year when they scattered, enjoying their time off. At least those who weren't teaching summer school.

And besides, none of her friends knew her secret about

Adam. Only Anna and Ray Collier—her parents' friends who befriended her when she arrived in the Chicago area, pregnant and alone—knew, but they were across the world living as missionaries right now.

Clouds hovered overhead, and Nicole hoped she didn't end up caught in an afternoon rain shower. When she turned the corner to River Street, she marveled at the wide river that paralleled the busy thoroughfare through town. Hawks Valley had become a big tourist destination as they boasted Woodvale Lodge, nestled in a great location alongside the river on the outskirts of town. Woodvale thrived on being one of the biggest wedding destinations in the South. Nicole hadn't been to the lodge in forever but hoped to make a trip there before she went back to Lincoln Park. Some of the grandchildren of the Woodvales had continued the tradition of managing the lodge.

The bell tinkled as she entered the coffee shop. Slight disappointment set in as she saw a teenage girl behind the counter instead of Rachel. Nicole ordered, then received her drink and sat at a table for two, sipping her hot liquid.

She glanced at her phone again, hoping for a text from Gavin.

Nothing.

"Hi, Nicole."

Nicole looked up, surprised yet hopeful, to see Rachel. "Hi. Do you have a minute to sit?" She doubted the busy coffee shop owner had time, but Nicole could use a friend.

Rachel shook her head. "No. I have to make a delivery. But come with me. We can chat in the car." Rachel turned, motioning for Nicole to follow. She looked down at her cutoff shorts and dusty pullover, then shrugged her shoulders. If the other woman didn't care what she was wearing, she wouldn't either. Nicole followed until they reached Rachel's car, where the coffee shop owner set a bag full of delicious smelling confections in the backseat. "Hey, do you mind holding these coffees?"

"Not at all. Glad I can help."

After sliding into the front seat, Rachel handed Nicole a tray with four coffees, their brown stoppers keeping all the heat in.

Rachel turned on the car, air conditioning blowing, and started driving. "You're selling your house, right? How's everything going?"

When other people said the words, selling sounded like a bad thing. But it was necessary. She couldn't stay here with Adam and his family around every corner. His mom was still too nice, his daughter completely adorable. And Adam, well, still handsome and kind and everything she'd left that long ago summer. "Yes, I'm selling. Living here isn't in my future."

Rachel shook her head. "I'm sorry to hear that. Hawks Valley is a small town, but I love it here. I left for a while, too. But when my sister died, I came back. Mom and Dad needed me. Then the coffee shop came up for sale as the owner was retiring, so I took my savings and bought it."

"I'm sorry to hear about your sister."

"Thank you. It was hard. But my niece Kylie and I get along great and see each other a lot. I'm still close to the Hawks—my sister's husband's family."

Kylie? Hawks? A chill ran through Nicole's veins as she held the hot coffee tray. "Do you mean Kylie Hawk?"

Rachel whipped a quick glance at Nicole. "Yes. Do you know her? And Adam?"

Why was this happening? How can the only girl that befriended her not only be Rebecca's sister, but be related to Adam through marriage? If Rachel was a part of Kylie's life, then she'd be a part of Gavin's life, too. No way could Nicole blurt out all of this, so she went with the obvious. "Yes. Adam and I went through school together."

"With Rebecca. I was a few years behind you guys. You probably don't remember me."

Nicole shook her head. "There's not much I remember from those school days."

Rachel shot Nicole a smile. "I get it. But still, how fun is it that you're here now. Have you seen Adam since you've been back?"

Simply by omission, she continued the secret. But since Shelley and Kylie didn't know yet, Rachel couldn't be told. Talk about tangled webs. "Yes. Shelley brought over food. You know how hospitable she is. Her famous chicken salad and lemon pound cake still rock."

"That's a win-win combination. I've tried to hire her to make lemon pound cake for me to sell, but she says she doesn't have time. She's always doing something for somebody it seems."

"Same Shelley, then." At least for now. At least until she and Adam sprung the news about Gavin on her. Then who knows what would take place. "Does she still love Christmas?"

Rachel nodded. "She still throws that amazing holiday party every year."

Nicole blew out a quick breath. "I remember my parents always went to the Hawks' annual Christmas party. That was the one event my dad went to even after my mom passed away. 'You never miss a Shelley Hawk Christmas party,' he used to say."

Rachel laughed. "It's still the same. So, tell me about you. What do you do for a living? Are you married? Children?"

Heat rushed over Nicole at the questions and deception they prompted. Maybe coming to town hadn't been such a good idea. She had made herself publicly accessible in a town she'd hidden secrets from for a long time. "I never married and I'm a schoolteacher in Lincoln Park, Illinois. I teach elementary-aged children. I really love my job."

Rachel smiled. "That's awesome. It takes a special person to be a teacher. Too bad you aren't staying longer. Kylie needs help in reading. She's a sweet girl, and smart, too. But reading isn't her strong suit. And if you don't grasp that, well, school can be challenging. I am right about that, aren't I?"

Nicole flushed again. Gavin had trouble reading when he was her age as well. She'd taken extra time with him at night, reading books and teaching him how to sound out words. In time, he became an avid reader. "Yes. Literacy is so important. Maybe Kylie could have a tutor over the summer to help her before she starts the new school year."

Rachel nodded, turning on her blinker. "That's a great idea. We'll have to relay that to Adam."

Nicole shook her head. *"We?"*

The other woman looked at her, a sly glance coming over her pretty features. "Yes. We'll be seeing him in a minute. We're taking these coffees to the airport. Clients flying out want coffee and snacks for the flight."

Panic began to grip Nicole, but she took a deep breath, hoping Rachel didn't notice. "Well, I'm not dressed to show up delivering anything. I'll wait in the car while you take this stuff in."

Rachel shook her head. "Nonsense. I'm sure you remember the private airport is small. Adam manages it now. No one cares what you're wearing. We're one big family."

One big family I left twenty-five years ago. And she took one family member with her. With all the fuss being made regarding the sale of the Victorian, Nicole couldn't imagine the talk when the folks of Hawks Valley learned about Gavin. Why had she ever thought this was a good idea? She had a good and simple life in Lincoln Park. Not always easy, but—until his accident—nothing she and Gavin couldn't push through together.

She swallowed hard at her son's silence. Not knowing where he was, especially with him in the precarious condition after the crash, had her worried. Her church upbringing told her that worry was a sin.

But she wasn't in that same place with God today. She remembered some scriptures, but she didn't rely on them anymore.

"Hawks Valley is one big family," Nicole agreed. But she had removed herself from the family category when she left at eighteen. And she didn't plan on staying here long enough to restore her status.

Adam finished entering his data in the app on the computer for the flight he was about to make. After this flight today, he had a light schedule until Sunday afternoon when he started flying guests back home from a wedding happening over the weekend.

Which suited him just fine. He missed Kylie. Between his mom and Rachel helping when she could, he didn't worry about his little girl when he had to fly. Occasionally he had to stay out of town overnight, but that didn't happen too often. He was thankful his job let him live a fairly normal life.

Adam never forgot to Whom the praise went regarding his life. He knew God directed steps and guided paths. Yet he had to admit that this path with Gavin had him baffled.

Why now? Twenty-four years without knowing his

son. A part of him said he should be angry, but another part was thrilled over the fact that he had a son. Incredible as it was, confusion set in as well.

What would he say to his son when he met him? He didn't believe Gavin would stay away long. After all, he knew firsthand how hard the information was to believe and digest. But once the reality of the situation sank in, Gavin would return. Hopefully curiosity, at least, would entice him to want to meet his father.

And he was a pilot.

"What's shakin', Hawk?"

Adam, almost to the hangar door, stopped. Only one person called him Hawk. Riles Maddox. He'd been a pilot here longer than Adam had been alive, and he'd be retiring soon. Riles and Paul, Adam's father, had been good friends and Adam knew Riles had been devastated at Paul's death.

Riles had been a big part of Adam not abandoning his dream of becoming a pilot. The two of them had plenty of talks in the sky about Paul and flying. Riles knew every hurt and joy that made up Adam.

Until now.

"I'm about to take a family back after their Woodvale vacation," Adam told him. "Super light schedule after this until the wedding guests start heading home. How about you?"

"Taking it easy for the most part. Everything okay?"

Of course Riles would pick up on his tension. Riles may be up there in age, but nothing got by him. "It's going. A blip on the radar you could say."

"Wanna talk about it?"

Did he? He hadn't even told his mom or Kylie about Gavin. But he needed some of this weight lifted off his chest. He knew his mom would be all kinds of emotional, and Kylie? He had no idea what to expect from her. "Maybe. Do you have a minute?"

"Sounds like we'll need more than a minute. I'm game. Let's have a seat."

Adam followed the older pilot to his small office in the hangar. Riles sat outside his office door, his chair in front of a card table where he worked a puzzle. Riles always had a puzzle going. People would come by and place pieces now and then. "Have a seat." Riles pointed to the only other chair across the table.

Riles made Adam comfortable. The man had worn the same cowboy boots and baseball hat for years. He'd be missed when he retired. Who would take over his office? Would there still be a working puzzle all the time?

Riles picked up a puzzle piece, examining it. "I'd like to think myself a good listener." He placed the puzzle piece next to another one, but it didn't quite fit.

"I have a son." Blurting the words seemed the best way to start.

Riles, a no-nonsense, get to the point kind of guy, looked at him, then nodded. "Okay. There's more to the story than that."

Adam spent the next few minutes relaying what had happened with Nicole's visit. "And Gavin left, thinking I didn't want to have anything to do with him. I haven't told my mom or Kylie yet." He looked Riles in the eye. "But he's a pilot. My son is a pilot."

"You gotta love how God works, Hawk. You know?" Riles continued to look between the puzzle piece in his hand to the work in progress on the table.

"Adam. I brought your order."

The thick tension of life changing words broke at the sound of Rachel's voice. Adam had forgotten about the delivery. Maybe she wouldn't linger, and he could continue his conversation with Riles.

Laughter rang through the hangar and Adam turned. Rachel had company.

Nicole.

She carried the tray with the coffees, sheepishly looking toward him.

"Adam. Look who I brought. Your long, lost friend, Nicole. Where do you want all of this?" Rachel held up a bag while she pointed to the tray Nicole held.

Adam motioned to an empty chair near the table with the puzzle. "Just set it there."

He watched the two ladies approach the table and had to admit that Nicole held his gaze with her simple attire and girl-next-door prettiness.

"Aren't you even going to say hello to Nicole?" Rachel elbowed Nicole.

Surely Rachel wasn't matchmaking, Adam thought. She had no idea at how that would never work out. "Hi, Nicole. Good to see you."

"Adam." She half smiled, but her tone rang with how uncomfortable this situation was.

Riles stood, holding out his hand. "Riles Maddox. Nice to see you again, Nicole. It's been a mighty long time."

Nicole nodded as she shook hands with Riles in what seemed like the longest handshake ever. Riles wasn't subtle. At all.

"Nice to see you again, too." Nicole shot a glance at Adam. A glance that said that she knew that Riles knew.

Rachel held up her phone as it started buzzing. "I have to take this. I'll be right back." She jaunted toward the front, her voice fading with each step.

Adam clasped his hands together, looking at Nicole.

"Yes, Riles knows. He's my mentor. I needed advice." He turned. "And you, old man, can't hold water. But that bucket better get plugged—at least until I tell my mom and Kylie."

Riles tried once again to place the puzzle piece but it didn't fit. "No hole here." He picked up another piece, setting the first one back on the table, his gaze glancing from Nicole to Adam. "You said he'd been in a crash and won't fly. Sounds like someone I knew a long time ago."

Adam's face heated. As a young boy he'd spent as much time in the air as on the ground. Then, after his father's crash, he refused every offer Riles made to take him flying. He'd cancelled his first round of lessons. "I remember. I can certainly talk to Gavin, but only the Lord knows what is in store, if he'll fly again." Adam stood. "I've said as much to Nicole."

Nicole's eyelashes fluttered. "I had no idea how you handled your father's death. I just knew you were flying. And that you somehow came through that tragedy. And that maybe, just maybe, you could help Gavin."

"Help Gavin how? And who's Gavin?"

Even though Rachel now stood next to Nicole, her voice seemed to resound loudly through the hangar, just as Adam's watch alarm went off. His clients would be arriving in five minutes.

Great.

At least the coffee would still be hot.

Chapter Five

Nicole ripped her hair from its ponytail, then fluffed it out with her hands. *"Ugh. What are you doing?"* Talking to herself wasn't normal behavior, but nothing was normal in her life right now. She'd spent most of the day in the garage, and after the fiasco yesterday at the airport with Riles and Rachel both finding out about Gavin, she and Adam had agreed that she would come over tonight to tell his mother.

Why did I put on makeup?

And what about the perfume she'd sprayed on her wrists? Simply a force of habit. Right? Once again, she wrapped the ponytail holder around her hair and practically ran out of the bathroom so she would stop messing with her appearance.

Adam. Childhood friend. Brief high school boyfriend. Father of her son. None of those things stopped him from being handsome. Facts were facts. And it's not like they were going to be on a date. Even so, she looked down at her denim capris and cute red sandals, the white-and-red, polka-dot shirt she wore complimented them perfectly.

Wanting to look nice wasn't a crime. It didn't mean anything. He said he would pick her up at six and hadn't mentioned anything about dinner. But she hadn't felt like eating much since Gavin left. She had received a couple of "I'm fine" texts, but she still had no idea where he fled or when or if he would be coming back to Hawks Valley.

Those thoughts made her stomach sink. She still texted him inspiring quotes like she had been doing since the crash, trying to keep things routine.

But everything had changed.

The knock on the door caused her to grab her purse. Shelley would probably want to see pictures of Gavin, so Nicole made sure she had her phone. She opened the door, ready to start another leg of this journey. Then sucked in a small breath at the sight of Adam. His gray shirt was tucked perfectly into his jeans, his cowboy boots proving certain attire never went out of style. Time had been good to him. "I'm ready," she said when he didn't move.

He nodded. "You look really nice."

Even at forty-three she blushed at his words, then wondered why. *Nice.* Not pretty or beautiful. This is what over emotionalism did to a person. "Thank you. You clean up well, too."

He took a step back as she walked out, pulling the door behind her, making sure it shut tight. The door she didn't dare lock at the prospect of Gavin's return.

"Where's the book?" Adam asked.

She pressed her hand against her chest, her breathing erratic. "It's in the house. Why?"

"I want to show my mom."

She shook her head. "You can't. It's personal and I'm not ready to share it with people." Her gaze bore into his confused one. "You read the words, right? They were written from a raw and tender place, specifically for you."

He shrugged. "I get that. But we're talking about my mom. Not the postman or grocery store clerk."

Why didn't he understand? Those were her life words, practically written in blood on those pages. All the dreams and angst of an eighteen-year-old girl, through her twenties, then thirties, journaling from the deepest places in her heart. Like a diary. These waters regarding Gavin were still too uncharted to share that book with anyone. "I'm not against your mom seeing it ever, just not tonight."

He held his hands out, palms up, the confused look still on his face. "All right."

She followed him down the stairs, then halted at the bottom as she spotted his red pickup truck "I still can't believe you drive the same truck you had in high school."

"I have a responsible dad car for taking Kylie around, but no way could I part with Rowdy Red. Still runs like a dream. And Kylie loves riding in her now and then."

Memories she'd pushed aside the first day she saw the truck flooded Nicole now. Hanging out in the parking lots, truck bed down, chatting with friends after pep rallies. Youth group trips from the church to River Pizza or the ice cream shop where several kids would climb in the back. "You remember the Memorial Day Parade when the little kids from the flag football team insisted you drive them? All the parents were beyond nervous."

"Sure. They named their team the Rowdy Reds. They still exist. I coach them every fall."

Of course he did. Adam Hawk couldn't be more ingrained in this town. Her heart skipped a beat, wondering how Gavin would fit into this small town life. "I'm nervous, Adam."

"Me, too." He opened the passenger door for her, another reminder of how polite and gentlemanly he had always been. Some things never changed.

He backed out of her driveway and took the familiar

route to his house. "It was nice of Rachel to offer to take Kylie so we could break the news to my mom first. Telling them together wouldn't be a good thing. Although I wouldn't put a matchmaking angle past Rachel."

Nicole sucked in a breath hoping Adam was joking. "That would be a waste of time and effort on her part."

Adam shrugged. "That's Rachel. Even though I hadn't planned on her knowing so soon, it's working out. Kind of like a sign from God, don't you think?"

It didn't surprise Nicole that Adam would bring up the Lord. "I don't think much about God."

"Whoa. That's a change. We had the best times in youth group and Sunday services."

"Yeah, well, when none of your prayers are answered, you start to wonder if anyone is listening." She didn't need a lecture from Adam regarding her spirituality, or lack of it, and breathed a sigh of relief when he didn't respond.

Her relieved feeling didn't last long, however, as she watched his strong arms turn the steering wheel, his biceps peeking out of his gray shirt. Combine that with the nostalgia of his old truck, the still-too-attractive Adam in the driver's seat, and her mind whirled. She needed to ground herself before seeing Shelley Hawk. Nicole kept looking at her phone, hoping for another text from Gavin.

Nothing.

Adam turned into his mom's driveway and Nicole noticed that the garden was still yard-of-the-month-worthy. Nicole sat, her leg bouncing with nervousness, knowing Adam would open her door. She let him help her out of the truck, his hand barely resting on her back as he guided her to the front door. His gentle touch normally would have rattled her, but the circumstances for this visit had done that pretty well on its own.

He didn't knock, just reached around her and opened the door, motioning her in ahead of him.

"Mom. We're here."

"In the kitchen, honey."

Stiffly Nicole walked by Adam's side, the familiarity of the house giving her strength. There had been some updates done, but Shelley's signature style still made one feel at home immediately. If only the reason for her visit wasn't filled with the unknown. They entered the kitchen and Nicole's gaze quickly landed on the table, which had been set for three. Her already knotted stomach clenched further at the smell of an amazing dinner drifting into her senses. Shelley, wearing a flowered apron over her clothes, hugged Adam first, then swept Nicole into a hug.

"Honey," Shelley said, backing away. "You're so tense. I know selling the Victorian is weighing on you, but you don't have to do a thing until you're ready."

"Mom, she cleaned out the garage all day. She's selling."

Adam sounded eager to have her out of town. Did he think she would hinder any time he wanted to spend with Gavin if she stuck around? Nicole wished she could back out the door and have a deeper conversation with Adam before they told Shelley the news.

This already awkward situation became more so with the table set and the expectation of dinner sitting on the stove and in the oven. The bread basket with the red-and-white checkered cloth draped over the sides waited for whatever yumminess would inhabit the basket. Nicole didn't know how she would refuse Shelley's famous, made-from-scratch rolls if that's what she was serving.

"I hope you two are hungry. I think I've made enough to feed an event at Woodvale, but it's just us three. No worries. I'll send both of you home with leftovers." As she finished speaking, she grabbed two pot holders, then pulled out the perfected rolls Nicole had feared.

The smell alone would win a blue ribbon. Nicole looked at Adam, her eyes pleading for an intervention.

Instead of rescuing her, he smiled. It sent her over the edge she had been perched on since he showed up at her door. Or maybe even earlier, when she realized she tailored her appearance to the fact that she would be seeing him tonight. If this tension wasn't resolved soon, Nicole felt like she would snap. "Shelley… Adam and I need to talk to you."

"But our talk can wait until after dinner." Adam couldn't push the words out fast enough. He kept his gaze focused on his mom, knowing any look he would give Nicole wouldn't be pleasant. Not that they had a plan of how they were going to approach the subject of Gavin with his mom, but, no doubt, the elaborate dinner threw both of them off.

Shelley placed the rolls into the basket and Adam could see the half curve of a smile she might be trying to hide. He had to head her thoughts off of where he knew they were going. "Mom, we're not a couple. Just putting that out there so we can have a nice dinner."

His mom covered the still steaming rolls before handing him the basket. "Would you set this on the table, please? And Nicole, do you mind filling our glasses? I have iced tea and water. I'll take tea."

"Me, too." Adam watched as Nicole, still refusing to meet his gaze, filled the glasses. Within a couple of minutes the fried chicken, mashed potatoes, gravy, green beans and macaroni and cheese joined the rolls on the table.

"Nicole, you can sit here." Shelley pointed to Kylie's normal seat. "Adam will you say the blessing?"

The sound of the kitchen faucet dripping seemed like a scream as he gathered his thoughts. "Dear Father. We thank You for Your provision, Your grace, Your abundance. Let our words be glorifying to You and open our hearts to receive all Your good gifts. Bless this food to our bodies, and our bodies to Your service. Amen."

"What a nice prayer, honey." Shelley took a piece of fried chicken before passing the platter. After the jostling of all the bowls, serving dishes, and bread basket, Adam looked at Nicole's plate. Barely enough for a bird. But he knew for a fact that she grabbed the biggest roll.

His mom wouldn't understand Nicole's lack of wanting to eat, but he did. His appetite hadn't been up to par lately either, but at least he was in familiar surroundings and he knew where his daughter was.

Unlike Nicole, who didn't know her son's whereabouts. She looked calm and cool on the outside, but her insides must be in turmoil. The few bites of chicken rumbled in his stomach at the thought. His son, too. Nicole pushing her little bit of food around her plate made sense. Her actions also reiterated what he needed to do.

"Mom. This is an incredible meal. But I'm afraid Nicole and I aren't in a position to appreciate it like it deserves." There. He'd started the conversation. Slight relief flowed through him but the next words seemed to stick in his throat.

Shelley put her fork down. "Okay. Talk. But just remember good news deserves key lime pie and there's no news bad enough that key lime pie can't cure. There's one waiting for us in the fridge."

He couldn't fault his mom for her words. Food had been her comfort for as long as he could remember. Cooking, eating and sharing a meal made up Shelley Hawk's coping mechanism.

"I guess there's only one way to say this, so I'm just going to say it. I, we—" he motioned between Nicole and himself "—we have a child. His name is Gavin. He's twenty-four years old."

Immediate tears streamed down Shelley's face, causing Adam to hold back his own tears, although the throaty way he delivered the news gave his emotional state away. His mom's left hand covered his right one, while her free hand wiped her eyes.

Nicole stood to grab a tissue from the counter.

Shelley dabbed her eyes. "This is more than a one tissue conversation. Grab the box, please. And tell me everything. Although, I'm in such shock, I'm not sure how much I'll remember." She shot him an agonizing look. "Adam, I know I'm supposed to forgive, but not telling me for all these years is pushing my limit."

Nicole set the box of tissues down and took a seat closer to his mom. "Adam didn't know. Not until a couple of days ago. And I don't expect to be forgiven, so it's okay."

Adam's heart ached at Nicole's words. He couldn't fathom living with that expectation, or lack thereof.

"Why have you kept this boy from us all these years, Nicole? I don't understand."

"The decision wasn't easy and wasn't made lightly. I agonized every day over whether I had made the right choice. I tried twice to tell Adam, but neither time worked out and—I don't know?—it felt like God kept closing doors, so I locked them I guess. Until now."

Nicole's words were basically the same as she told him. They seemed gentler towards his mom. Or maybe because they weren't surprising to him this time, they just sounded that way. "I'm still in shock, too, Mom. Of course I have to tell Kylie. I could use some prayers regarding that conversation."

"Here's his picture." Nicole handed her phone to his mom, whose hand trembled as she gazed at the screen, her head moving back and forth. "He's Adam all over."

She dabbed her eyes again which still spouted tears. "He's beautiful. Can you text me this picture?"

"Sure. I'll get your number from Adam."

"So where is he? Is he here…in town?" Her tear-filled gaze bounced from Adam to Nicole.

Adam shook his head. "No. That's another problem. He surprised Nicole by coming early, and he saw—" Adam quickly remembered the book and how Nicole wanted to keep that between them for now. "He found out about me and left."

Shelley's mouth gaped open. "You mean all this time he didn't know about you either?"

"No. But Nicole and I are giving him time to cool off. Process this. We're sure he'll be back soon."

Once again the faucet dripped loudly as Shelley continued to wipe beneath her eyes. "I can't believe this. Of all the things I could imagine in my mind, never did I envision this news. And, young lady—" Shelley turned to Nicole "—I can't for the life of me understand your reasoning regarding this situation. You've kept a young man away from not only his father, but a loving extended family. We could have been a part of his life all these years. Now apparently he's scared to even come around. I'm disappointed and hurt and many other things I can't express at this moment. I'm not sure there's a way to right this wrong." She pushed her chair back, then picked up her plate.

"Looks like it's a good time for that key lime pie." Adam's heart hurt, but the mood needed lightening big time.

Shelley scraped her uneaten food into the trash can before setting her plate in the sink. "I take back what I said. There *is* news that key lime pie won't fix."

Adam scooted his chair back and reached his mom quickly. He wrapped her in his arms. "It's okay, Mom. I know Gavin will come around. He'll meet us all. It might take a little while, but we'll be a family." Shelley returned the hug before ending the embrace.

He took a couple of steps toward Nicole, who had stood up and now stared out the window, her back to them. Torn between these two women, his love for his mom and his mixed feelings for Nicole, he halted his steps knowing even though she was hurting, she wouldn't be receptive to his comfort.

Nicole turned, her face void of expression or tears. "I'd never keep Gavin from any of you."

The irony of her statement stirred his already unstable emotions, piquing an obviously underlying ire. "You've kept him from us for twenty-four years, Nicole."

His words bit. He could tell by the way she flinched. Her slight movement solidified the space between them. The light mood he feigned earlier had been a front. The short amount of days knowing he had a son had him reeling in all areas. Frustration ruled right now over everything.

His stance also proved that nothing came between a son and his mom. He needed to remember that. This situation with Gavin was delicate at best. People's lives were at stake. Hearts were at risk.

"You've done us a disservice, Nicole, keeping a young man from his father. I see why you're eager to sell the Victorian. Rid yourself of all the reminders of the hometown you grew up in, yet deprived your son, my grandson, of all those memories. Time will heal this, but not without repercussions, I'm afraid." Shelley sighed. "Now

I'm going to pack up this food and run it over to the Masons. They had a baby girl last weekend, and they'll enjoy this food even though we didn't."

Nicole crossed her arms. "I didn't mean to make such a mess of things. I did what I thought was best at the time for my son. I've always put his interests first. That's why I'm here now, subjecting myself to all kinds of talk, possible rejection. None of it matters if Gavin is healed and flying soon."

"Healed?" His mom had every reason to be confused.

"He's a pilot, Mom. He was in a plane crash. He's physically fine, but mentally won't bring himself to fly. Nicole thought I might have some influence on him."

Nicole put her hands on the back of the chair. "I still have confidence you will. When we all come to terms with everything and when time has, like Shelley said, healed us."

Adam swallowed hard. Everyone had a different way of navigating these troubled skies. Right now they were crisscrossing, pushing through the storm clouds. His mom was hurt beyond what he could have imagined. Why didn't he see that coming?

Meanwhile, Nicole stood her ground like a mama bear guarding her cub, and why wouldn't she?

And Adam fell somewhere in between elation and hurt, guarded yet wanting to know everything about Gavin. Adam now saw Nicole's discernment when it came to the book. It wasn't the right time.

Maybe all of her decisions weren't to be questioned. Maybe there was validity to her reasoning. But one thing was certain. From this point forward, he would be involved in decisions regarding Gavin.

Nicole wouldn't deprive him of helping to decide what was best for his son.

Chapter Six

Nicole woke, hoping last night had been a nightmare.

It hadn't been.

That ride home in Adam's truck, which had lost any sense of nostalgia, had seemed like hours instead of minutes. She'd pushed open her door before he fully stopped in her driveway, murmuring good-bye as she fled.

Fled the wolves.

Or at least a she-wolf in Shelley Hawk's case.

Nicole threw on some running clothes and took to the street, her feet pounding her frustrations and guilt into the sidewalk.

After torturing herself for over an hour, she slowed her pace to a walk, making her way into town. A nice coffee, a smile and a kind word from Rachel might put her in a better mood. The café owner hadn't chided her or questioned her motivation regarding Gavin on the drive from the airport yesterday.

Instead, she had just been supportive and offered a listening ear.

Once inside The Morning Grind, she again gave her order to a teenage girl. Setting up a pay device on her phone had its benefits, indicating Nicole was capable of making good decisions. Even if she'd been mentally revisiting all the ones she made regarding Gavin.

"I'll bring your muffin out to you after I heat it," the girl, whose name tag read *Holly*, said.

"Great. Thank you."

"Nicole! Over here."

Nicole smiled at the sound of Rachel's voice, but the smile left when she saw who sat with her.

Kylie.

Nicole never would have imagined Rachel bringing Adam's daughter to work with her.

"Come over and sit with us."

To refuse would be nothing short of rude. Especially since she told Holly she was eating her muffin here and it would be served on a real plate. "Sure. I'd love to."

Nicole walked over as Rachel pulled out a chair with a sweet smile on her face. "Have a seat. Kylie and I were just working on her reading, weren't we?"

Kylie nodded, her expression anything but thrilled. "Do you like to read?" Nicole asked the little girl who resembled her dad in so many ways, even though she had Rebecca's facial features.

Kylie shrugged. "Not really. It's hard."

The chapter book sitting in front of Kylie looked brand new. Nicole tapped the book cover. "Cinderella. I love that fairy tale."

Kylie shifted in her seat, her little legs moving a mile a minute underneath the chair. "I like to watch the movie or have someone read the story to me."

Because it was hard, Nicole surmised. "Reading can be fun. I teach children like you how to read."

"Kylie. Nicole is a school teacher." Rachel focused on Nicole. "Kylie and I have been praying for a sweet teacher to help her learn to read over the summer like you suggested."

Nicole wanted to believe in prayer like all these people. But she just couldn't.

"I like Miss Nicole. Maybe you could help me?" Kylie took a bite of her cookie, her head bopping back and forth to the music overhead.

Ice shot through Nicole at the thought of spending more time than necessary with any of the Hawks. Especially little girls who reminded her of their daddy, and who could steal her heart if she let them.

"Miss Nicole isn't staying all summer, Kylie. We probably have to pray for someone else." Rachel's hooded glance begged a denial—one Nicole couldn't give.

"Here's your muffin." Holly slid the plate in front of Nicole.

"Thank you." Although now, she had lost her appetite. *Again*.

"And Rachel," Holly hesitated. "I hate to bother you but they're delivering a ton of items and since I'm new, I don't want to sign for them without you checking everything. I'm sorry."

Rachel stood. "Nicole, can you keep an eye on Kylie for a few minutes? Actually, Adam will be here soon to pick her up." She made no attempt to hide her huge smile. Could Adam be right? Could Rachel be a matchmaker in disguise?

This is what it felt like to be backed into a corner. "Sure. I've got it."

"Thanks." Rachel and Holly left, leaving Nicole sitting across from Kylie. Nicole's phone dinged. A text from Gavin. Her face flushed. Just a good morning message, but Nicole considered that progress. She quickly texted a good morning back, adding an *I love you* with a heart emoji.

"Who are you texting?" Kylie asked.

Your half brother. The coffee shop had turned into dangerous territory. "A friend." It wasn't a lie. Her son was her friend.

"I miss my friends in the summer. I see them sometimes, but I like when we go to school so I can see them every day. I just don't like reading." Kylie shoved the last of the cookie in her mouth, then took a drink out of a cup similar to Nicole's.

"Are you drinking coffee?" Nicole knew she wasn't, but at least the subject would be safe.

Kylie giggled. "No. I'm not allowed to have coffee. This is yummy hot chocolate."

"I like hot chocolate, too. Look on the side of your cup. Do you see the word 'hot'?"

Kylie turned her cup around, scrunching up her face. "I don't know."

"Look real good. I'm sure you can find it."

Kylie's finger traced the area where the label had printed.

Nicole moved seats so she could see Kylie's label. "Do you see the letter H? Two sticks going up and down then a smaller one right between, connecting them."

"Here?" Kylie's face scrunched.

Nicole nodded. "Yes. Then next to it is an O."

"H, O."

Nicole pointed to the next letter. "And a T. H-O-T. Hot."

Kylie started with her finger at the H. "H-O-T. Hot! I did it! I readed it."

"Read it, but yes. You did. Now that wasn't so hard, was it?"

Kylie shrugged again, but this time a smile graced her face. "Daddy!"

Kylie's chair nearly tipped over as she scooted it away from the table and ran to Adam, who scooped her up into his arms. Tears welled in Nicole's eyes. Had she made a mistake in not telling Adam about Gavin sooner?

Her mind reached back to the only other time she had snuck back to Hawks Valley. Gavin was three. She had driven in on a Friday night to see her father and left Sunday morning. A quick, but fun visit. She had toyed with the idea of telling Adam then. But her father didn't even know Adam was Gavin's father. So when she thought of everyone and everything that would change, those thoughts overwhelmed her still young, and probably immature, mind, and she drove back to Lincoln Park secret still intact. Besides, Adam had been married for years then. Nicole was convinced he hadn't thought about her once.

Nicole rubbed her arms, the air suddenly chilled. She couldn't let a woman, even a smart, caring woman like Shelley Hawk, have her second guessing every decision. Until the crash, Gavin was a well-established, hardworking young man. He had a college education and had dated, but no one seriously. Her son surrounded himself with good friends, and he loved to play rec soccer with them. His life had just hit some turbulence right now.

"Hi, Nicole."

Adam's tone bordered between welcoming and annoyed. As he stood over her, he held Kylie in his arms.

"Hi. I was just leaving." She started to scoot her chair back.

"You lefted your muffin. And you haven't finished helping me read the word after 'hot.'" Kylie wiggled out of Adam's arms, then dropped to the ground. She pushed her chair next to Nicole's, stopping any escape, and grabbed her cup. "Here. Help me with this word. Daddy, can Miss Nicole help me learn to read until she has to go away?"

The look on Adam's face made her wish there was a hole in the floor that she could slip through. "Rachel mentioned that I was leaving town before the summer was over."

"After Aunt Rachel said that, Miss Nicole taught me how to read the word 'hot' from the label on my cup. She's a good teacher. Even if it's only for a little while."

Adam slid into Rachel's chair, his gaze never leaving Nicole's, like he was trying to assess the situation, or her motives.

Of which she had none.

Honestly, she walked in the door looking for coffee and a friend. A friend that now knew her secret. And here she sat with Adam and his daughter. She did have her coffee and uneaten muffin. And a teaching side gig if Kylie had her way.

Which by Adam's tone and body language, she wouldn't.

"I'm sure you'll find someone here that can help you for the summer. But do you know I teach in Lincoln Park, Illinois, and I get to walk to school from my house? Even in the snow."

Kylie scrunched up her face. "I take a bus. Or Daddy or Grandma takes me. Mommy used to take me, but she's in heaven with Jesus now."

Nicole sucked in a breath at the child's honesty. "That's a special place to be."

Kylie nodded. "It is. Jesus loves all of us, but He wanted Mommy with Him now." She sipped her hot chocolate like she had just talked about coloring a paper or swinging on a swing.

"Did you have a good time with Aunt Rachel last night?" Adam asked Kylie.

"Yes. We always have fun. Then I had fun this morning with Miss Nicole." The six-year-old leaned her head against Nicole's arm—an intimate gesture for not knowing the girl very long. But Nicole didn't move. Not that Adam's gaze would let her. His gaze held her in place.

"We need to leave soon. Grandma is taking you swimming at Woodvale this afternoon. I know you'll love that."

Kylie slipped out of her chair and crawled in Adam's lap. "Yay! Fun! I love swimming. Maybe Miss Nicole wants to come? Grandma never gets into the water with me. But you would, wouldn't you, Miss Nicole?"

"Nicole probably has plans today." He sat straighter in his chair as if his words needed reinforcement.

"Your dad's right, I do have plans. But you'll have fun with your grandma." Although she really wanted to leave, she sat transfixed by the picture before her of Adam and his daughter. Nicole had robbed him of these precious moments with Gavin. Would Adam hold that against her? What if Gavin were here now? Would all three of them be sitting as a family? What was left of her heart broke at the thought of not being a part of the Hawk clan. She'd dreamed of it for so long, then came to reality eventually, but now, glimpses of what life might be like as a part of their family were literally unfolding before her eyes.

"Oh, Adam. You're here." Rachel walked up, pushing the empty chair closer to the table instead of sitting down. "I hope you don't mind me leaving Kylie with Nicole for a few minutes. I had to check in a large delivery."

"Everything's cool." Adam ruffled the top of Kylie's head.

"I thought it would be. Can I steal Kylie for five minutes? I need her help deciding which cupcakes to put out next."

"As long as she doesn't eat a cupcake. And hey, thank you for all the help with mom's surprise party. The church is set. Decorations have arrived and are being stored at the church. I really appreciate your help."

"No worries. The RSVPs are coming in fast and hard. Everyone loves Shelley Hawk. It will be quite the surprise. Come on, Kylie."

"Remember, no more cupcakes." Adam nodded at the cookie crumbs on the table.

"He's no fun," Rachel said as Kylie jumped down from Adam's lap. Rachel winked at Nicole before grabbing Kylie's hand as the two walked behind the counter to the back room.

She's a definite matchmaker, Nicole thought.

"You're still not eating?" Adam asked, pointing to her barely nibbled-on muffin.

"I'm not really hungry. How's your mom? Sounds like you're planning a party for her. I guess she needs it after last night." She'd never seen the version of Shelley she witnessed after they told her about Gavin. And honestly, Nicole thought she'd have an ally in Shelley.

Another illusion.

Adam tapped his fingers on the table. "She's like all of us. Surprised, confused, devastated…unsure how to proceed. And yes, Rachel and I are planning a surprise party for her seventieth birthday in a couple of weeks."

"That sounds like fun. Maybe it will cheer her up. I knew this wouldn't be easy, but I guess—"

"Yet, she's like me in that she can't wait to meet Gavin," he interjected. "I think we would all settle down if we knew when that was going to happen."

An outsider looking in would think they were having a completely normal conversation, not one that had rocked so many people's world. "Hopefully, soon. I miss him so much."

"I wish I knew what to miss." He leaned back in his chair, crossing his arms over his chest.

While his words weren't meant to be daggers, they stabbed Nicole to the core. Had she really thought this through? Like all her decisions, she wanted the best for Gavin. "I can't change the past, Adam. I can only move forward."

A muscle twitched in his jaw. "Have you heard from him?"

"Yes. He texted me good morning earlier. I see that as progress."

Adam sat straighter, his interest peaked. "That's awesome. I'm going to tell Kylie tonight. Me and mom."

Another family door slammed in her face, but she didn't blame him. Her suggestion of helping him tell Shelley had bombed big time. "That's good." And that would save her from any more reading lessons, as Kylie might see her as the enemy, too.

Late that afternoon, Adam turned down the long, tree-lined drive that led to the Woodvale Lodge, wishing he knew what ran through Nicole's mind. But she was female. He knew nothing about the female mind. His mom's reaction blew him away last night. After he took Nicole home, he returned and helped his mom pack up the food. He then drove her to the Masons. They had a long talk when they returned home as they cleaned the kitchen. By the time he needed to leave, his mom was nervous, but also anxious, to meet Gavin and welcome him to the family. Which is how Adam thought she would react. It just took a little time for everything to sink in.

The Woodvale parking lot didn't have many spaces left. He wasn't surprised as he just returned from flying in another couple for the wedding this weekend. A last minute addition to the guest list.

The flight had been good for him, because climbing the skies always cleared his mind. It gave him a fresh perspective and his sanity back. He needed that sanity before the conversation tonight with his daughter.

Children are resilient.

Riles's words echoed through Adam's mind. He prayed they would prove truthful in this situation. Hurting Kylie in any way would never be on his agenda. She'd already experienced more hurt than any six-year-old should, and she had come through it with, well, resilience.

Adam searched for a spot to park. When he landed, there had been a message from his mom stating her car wouldn't start and he needed to pick them up at Woodvale Lodge. He'd been warning her about her battery for a couple of weeks. Adam now had another item on his to-do list for tomorrow.

Spotting a sedan pulling out, he whipped his car into the spot. Woodvale boasted crowds from all over the country. The world, actually. The family-run lodge had kept up with the times while preserving the traditions from old. A winning combination when it came to important events like weddings, anniversaries, birthdays and such.

Adam waved and nodded to people he knew but strode to the pool area to retrieve Kylie and his mom. His resolve set, he wanted to have this conversation with his daughter behind him.

The five o'clock sun still shone brightly, glistening off the pool water. The crowd, probably thinned out from earlier, populated the pool and lounge chairs. He found

Shelley sitting at a table under a yellow-and-white Woodvale signature umbrella. Kylie sat next to her wrapped in a towel, spooning a slushy into her mouth.

"Hi, Mom. Y'all ready?"

"Grandma bought me a slushy while we were waiting on you. Her car is broken."

"Broken down," Adam corrected. "I'll come and put a battery in the car tomorrow, Mom."

"Thank you. I'm sorry I didn't take it in like you said, but it seems like there's never been a good time. And it wouldn't even start when that nice Woodvale employee tried to jump it off. Must be pretty dead." She stood, gathering items, shoving them in the pool bag.

"Or it's the alternator. Either way, it's all right. I'll check it out tomorrow. At least I don't have any flights."

"Oh, goody. We can play all day!" Kylie's blue slushy lips smiled at him.

Shelley shook her head. "I'm taking you to Mila's birthday party tomorrow afternoon. Remember the fun present we bought for her?"

"Oh, yeah. I forgot." Kylie picked up her shorts and shirt.

"Thanks for taking her, Mom. I'll fix the car first thing." Sweat furrowed his brow. His attire of a polo, jeans and boots didn't exactly scream pool-wear. He inched farther under the umbrella, handing his mom a pair of goggles. "I think this is everything."

Kylie shimmied into her pink shorts and unicorn shirt, and then slipped on her flip-flops. "I'm going to have fun at the party tomorrow, Daddy."

Tomorrow. Her world would have a different perspective by then. "I'm sure you will, sweetheart."

Adam draped her wet towel over his arm before shrugging the overfilled pool bag onto his shoulder. "Let's go, ladies."

Kylie giggled. "I'm a little girl, Daddy."

They made their way through the pool area and the lobby, then headed out to the parking lot to Adam's car, where he turned the air conditioner to high. Kylie buckled herself in, but before Adam could back out of the spot, Shelley put a hand on his arm.

"Wait a minute. I can't find my phone." She continued to dig in her purse. "I think I left it on the table."

"I'll get it, Mom. Be right back."

Adam jaunted through the lobby to the pool area and found the phone sitting on the table. He grabbed it and started to retrace his steps.

"Oh, hey, Adam."

He turned at the sound of the voice. Lark Woodvale had stopped and started walking toward Adam. "Hi, Lark. Everything okay?"

Lark's grandparents had built and opened Woodvale Lodge. Some of the family still worked here and Lark was the event planner while also teaching at the dance studio in the lodge. She even gave ballroom dance lessons for the upcoming newlyweds.

"Yes. Everything's great. Big wedding this weekend, though. Huge."

"I figured. I've flown in a lot of folks for it."

Lark smiled, her blue eyes sparkling. She'd always been a good friend, nothing more. "We love that the airport is so close. By the way, were you here earlier today?"

"Just a few minutes ago to pick up Kylie and my mom. Mom left her phone on the table, so I came back in to grab it."

Lark shook her head. "No. I mean this morning. There's a young man here who could have been your twin in high school. They say we all have a double somewhere. Strange that yours is running around Woodvale."

Adam's blood rushed through his veins. *Gavin.* Could his son be here? At Woodvale? "Thanks for letting me know. Maybe I'll run into him sometime."

He choked the words out, hoping Lark didn't notice. Holding up the phone, he said, "Good seeing you. I have to run, though."

"Take care, Adam."

His heart pounded hard as he looked left and right on his way back through the lobby and to the parking lot. Was Gavin really here? Could he have been at the pool? Close to his family? He knocked on the passenger side window and his mom opened the door.

"Mom. Something's come up." He cut his eyes to the backseat. "I can't talk about it now, but can you take Kylie to your house in my car? I'll get a ride to your house in a little while."

His mom's eyes softened. "Of course." Adam handed her the key he kept in his pocket. After kissing his mom on the cheek, he hugged her. "Thanks, Mom." He opened the back door. "I have to stay here for a little while, princess. Go home with Grandma and I'll see you there soon."

"Okay, Daddy." Kylie's soft voice and her heavy eyelids indicated she'd be napping during the drive. He kissed her forehead, whispered another thanks to his mom, then shut the door and jaunted to the front of the Woodvale Lodge. He pulled his phone out of his pocket and dialed Nicole.

"Hello?"

Her hesitant voice almost caught him off guard. "Hi. Are you at home?"

"Yes."

"How fast can you get to Woodvale?"

"I guess however long it takes me to drive there. Ten minutes? Why?"

"I think Gavin is here."

Adam watched Nicole park completely crooked in the spot that just opened in the first row. She flew out of the car, flushed but still beautiful. He'd been pacing ever since he'd hung up with her.

She ran up to him, his arms instinctively wrapping around her body. She rested against him for a moment, her flowery, clean scent enveloping him, transporting him to days gone by when springtime secrets led to the events of today.

He couldn't dwell.

Nicole stepped back. "Have you seen him?"

"No." Adam quickly relayed the conversation he had with Lark. "I've been in the parking lot. I can't believe how nervous I am."

"Let's go over here and sit for a minute." Nicole nodded to the black wrought iron benches surrounding a fountain at the front of the lodge. They were deserted. Perfect for their private conversation.

"What are you thinking? Besides finding your son. *Our* son." Adam still became mesmerized at the word "son." It still sounded strange coming from his mouth, like a foreign word.

"I'm not sure this is such a good idea."

He couldn't believe her words. "What do you mean? How can it not be a good idea?"

Nicole fiddled with the buttons on her blouse. "He said he needed time. If he's here, and we don't know that for sure, he didn't go far. I think it's important we give him his time to sort out everything. Us showing up here together might look like we're ganging up on him. Forcing him into something."

Adam stood, shoving his hands in his pockets. "I see what you're saying, but can't we at least go to the desk and ask if he's checked in? Then we'll know whether or not he's here."

She stood, looking unsure. "Then what? What if they say yes?"

"Wouldn't that give you some peace of mind, knowing where he is?"

"On one hand, yes. On the other hand, I feel like I'm spying. He's not a runaway teen, Adam. He's a grown man."

Frustration roiled through him, but Adam took a deep breath, focusing on the fact that Nicole knew Gavin and he didn't. "Okay. How about I go in by myself and find out if he's here. Then we can leave. But, if he is here, it will give us both peace of mind without him thinking you were spying on him. You just heard it from a friend."

She tilted her head. "*Are* we friends, Adam?"

He took in her pretty summer blouse and white shorts, her glittery-looking sandals and fresh face—void of makeup but beautiful enough to take a man's breath away. Her dark hair framed her face softly like it always had. "I think we're friends."

"There was a time when I thought we were more than friends, but I was mistaken. I can't put myself in that position again."

Regret, confusion and curiosity filled his mind. Nicole was complex on her own and adding Gavin made her even more complex. Here they stood, so close to finding Gavin yet so far from an actual meeting, never mind relationship. He needed to push any thoughts of a relationship with Nicole to the side and focus on eventually meeting his son. "I'm sorry for all that, Nicole. I can't go back and change my actions, but I can offer friendship now."

"This situation is awkward, Adam, but to be honest, I could use you as a friend."

He held out his hand, and she placed hers in his. Her fingers were soft, yet they gripped his like a lifeline. He'd unknowingly let her sink years ago. He couldn't do it again, even if a future with her would never come to pass "Can I go in?"

She nodded. "Let's go together."

They turned and started walking. She dropped his hand, the loss immediate, yet necessary. They threaded their way past the people in the lobby and approached the front desk.

"Can I help you?" A young girl wearing a dark blazer and a white shirt smiled at them.

"I hope so. Can you tell me if a Gavin Haw… St. John has checked in?" How quickly the last name Hawk almost slipped from his lips. Gavin, a Hawk by blood, was legally a St. John.

The girl nodded. "I can give you that information, but I can't tell you his room number or anything else."

Adam placed his hands on the marble counter, trying to still his nerves. "We understand."

Her fingers flew across the keyboard, but it seemed like a lifetime. "Ah, yes. I see a Gavin St. John is checked in."

Adam heard Nicole suck in a breath. "Gavin," she whispered.

"Thank you." Adam grabbed her hand as they backed away from the desk, each of them scanning the lobby.

"We need to leave," Nicole hissed close to his ear. "Now."

Once again, she let go of his hand as they passed

through the Woodvale Lodge lobby. He pushed through the wooden doors that had graced the lodge since its opening. The June heat hit him, but not as much as the knowledge that Gavin was near. He stopped, scanned the group of four that walked toward them. All blonds. He stood, rooted in place.

"Adam, come on." Nicole took his hand, then started walking, her grip tight in his as they reached her car.

It still seemed surreal to Adam. "He's here. Somewhere."

Nicole nodded. "Which means we'll hear from him soon. Trust me."

Trust her? Trust someone who had lied to him by omission for the last twenty-five years? He gave her hand a gentle squeeze, grounding himself in reality, before letting go, the irony of his predicament not lost on him. "I don't have any other choice."

Chapter Seven

"A big brother! Seriously? Are you telling the truth, Daddy?"

Adam couldn't help but smile at Kylie's innocence at the situation. "Yes, I am. His name is Gavin. He's not here right now, but he will be sometime soon."

Clapping her hands, Kylie danced around the kitchen. "I can't wait to meet him. When will I? How did you grow him so big, so fast?"

Adam glanced at his mom whose expression had visibly relaxed at Kylie's words. Shelley had a half smile on her face. "He grew on his own. Like you are. He's just been growing more years."

Kylie nodded. "Makes sense. Can I have the dessert Aunt Rachel gave me?"

"Sure," Adam said, surprised at how well this went. Riles had been right. Kids were resilient. And they don't carry all the baggage. His daughter had no concept of the full implications of Gavin coming into their lives.

Her view and reaction was refreshing and much-needed.

Now if he could just meet his son.

Those words came easier into the brain now. They still surprised but didn't jar. Only sheer force and his promise to Nicole prevented him from hanging out in the Woodvale lobby. He and Nicole may not be in total agreement about some things, but he respected her opinion and insistence in this matter.

Gavin was so close.

Time.

He reasoned that he would do this right to make it right. No sense acting rash and risk this relationship starting, then possibly ending, badly.

"What do you know about my big brother, Daddy?"

He looked over at Kylie who had whipped cream on her chin as she shoved another bite of cupcake in her mouth.

"He flies planes like I do."

"Where does he live? Will he live with us?"

Adam shook his head. "He lives in the state of Illinois right now. Remember he's older. He can have his own house, so he probably won't live with us."

Would living in Hawks Valley appeal to Gavin at all? The drive to Lincoln Park was eight hours. A flight would be shorter of course. And they were both pilots.

But Gavin wasn't flying right now. Nicole thought Adam would be a help in that department, but he had no idea about the crash or the exact reasons Gavin refused to fly. Adam thanked God his son had survived then remembered almost sidetracking his dream of becoming a pilot after his father's crash and death. Family and friends were a big help, Riles most of all.

"Mom, were you scared for me to be a pilot after dad's crash?" It just dawned on Adam that he had a wealth of information about this situation in his mom.

"I was terrified. But I trusted God."

"Did you ever think of telling me not to become a

pilot?" Adam slid into a chair across from his mom and Kylie at the table.

"The thought probably crossed my mind. There were so many things going on at that time. I busied myself to keep from thinking about it much. We were planning your wedding, remember?"

"The wedding to Mommy!" Kylie smiled.

Adam thought back to that time. How guilty he'd felt after stepping out on Rebecca even though they were broken up. Physically, that is. Heart-wise, he hadn't left her, and he should have considered that where Nicole was concerned. Although his growing feelings for Nicole added a whole level of confusion to his heart that he hadn't been prepared to deal with.

So he didn't.

He swallowed hard, remembering how he suspected Nicole had a crush on him. He liked her a lot as a friend, a really good friend. And of course he thought she was beautiful. Everyone did. And when they dated, hung out, whatever you wanted to call it for that month, his feelings toward Nicole evolved into more than a friendship. Those feelings scared him, so when Rebecca wanted him back, marriage seemed like the seal of redemption for him. Like it proved how much he loved Rebecca. After all, she had held his heart all those years. Why leave a familiar situation for one that was unsure?

Looking back, he easily saw the mind game he'd played. At the time, vulnerability over his father's unexpected crash, combined with the time away from Rebecca, drove his emotions when, in reality, he probably should have stepped back and evaluated more.

He should have looked inward more during his marriage as well. Maybe he would have seen that Rebecca was unhappy, but he had no clue. He thought the three of them were a happy family and that he and Rebecca were still in love.

Not so, according to her lawyer. She'd wanted a divorce. How could he have been so blind?

He wouldn't make that mistake again. Adam had poured all his energy into raising Kylie, and another romantic relationship had been the furthest thing from his mind. At least until Nicole had walked back into his life in the most unexpected way.

As the mother to his son.

And that's all she could be.

But if that were true, why did she keep invading his mind? Every time she did, he kept reminding himself that she hid a son from him. What else would she hide? He could never fully trust her. And a relationship without trust wasn't a relationship at all.

"I'm glad you didn't stop me, Mom. I love my job. I love flying. There's nothing like it to clear the mind."

"Your father used to say pilots were born, not made. He never wanted to do anything else."

Adam reflected on what Nicole had told him about Gavin. He'd gone behind her back to become a pilot. The pull had obviously been strong. But now, fear had set in for Gavin. And Nicole thought he could help. What if Gavin never had the accident?

A chill fell over Adam at the thought. It was all he could do to sit here and not stalk Woodvale to find him. But enough damage had been done. He had to rely on Nicole's judgment in this situation.

He couldn't risk not knowing his son.

Nicole woke on Saturday morning, her soul lighter. One by one, things were coming together. Even though she hadn't seen Gavin, knowing he was so close calmed her heart immensely.

But they had to give him time.

They being her and Adam. It fell all over her that sharing such intimate knowledge with Gavin's father bonded them. After all the years of feeling like she flew solo in caring for Gavin's well-being, she finally had a partner.

But only when it came to their son.

Although Nicole couldn't help but wonder what it would be like to be a family with Adam and Gavin. And Kylie, of course. It had been just her and Gavin for so long. The addition of more people seemed strange.

She missed her son yet understood his need to process the life-altering news. She wanted to hold him and tell him everything would be okay. But she couldn't guarantee that it would.

Nicole grabbed her coffee as she headed to the garage. She pushed the button and the garage door groaned its way upward, letting light and air into the space. A pile that would be going to the dump sat in the middle of the floor. She had two shelves and one closet to go.

A car pulled into the driveway and Mary, the real estate agent, exited the car. "Good morning, Nicole." Mary walked toward her holding a thick packet.

"Good morning."

"I have the contract for you to sign. I wanted to deliver it personally. We'll bring the 'For Sale' sign out later today or tomorrow. I know the Victorian will sell quickly. I have half a mind to buy it myself, it's so beautiful, but Ron would kill me."

Nicole followed Mary's glance toward the house. Beautiful and charming, it lived up to its stately name. A slight breeze blew a refreshing feel into the air. No humidity. A perfect day in Hawks Valley.

"I've marked all the places that need your signature." Mary handed her the golden envelope. "And I have a pen right here in my pocket."

The packet, feeling foreign and heavy in Nicole's hands, threatened to overwhelm her. A few swipes of Mary's fancy looking pen would start the process of ending her life in Hawks Valley. She'd thought so often about it and was so sure about her decision, but her hesitancy now confused her. "I'd like to read over these papers. Can I bring them to your office tomorrow?"

Mary cocked her head, holding tightly to the pen. "They are standard real estate contracts. Nothing hidden, I promise. My commission is the standard in the industry."

Nicole nodded. "I understand. I just want to look over them."

The realtor glanced at the house, then back to Nicole. "Of course. The office is closed Sunday but I can drop by. Just text me."

"Thank you for bringing the contracts by," Nicole said as Mary started walking to her car.

"You're welcome. See you tomorrow." She backed out of the driveway just as Adam pulled up.

He waved Mary on before taking her spot. "Get everything signed?" he asked, exiting his truck.

Nicole tried not to stare. Adam had always been handsome, but this older version of the boy she'd once adored seemed even more so. His faded jeans, dark blue T-shirt and well-loved boots would never go out of style for him. Gavin's resemblance to Adam couldn't be denied, yet their son had his own look. "I'm going to read them over and give them to her tomorrow." She nodded toward the thick packet.

"Good idea. Have you heard from Gavin?"

Ah, the real reason for the visit. "No. And I haven't changed my mind. We're not going to track him down."

Adam shut his door. "I know. It's just unnerving knowing he's so close."

"He stayed close for a reason. He doesn't want to run. He just needs to think. How did things go with Kylie?"

Adam smiled. "She was surprisingly excited. Kylie can't wait to meet her big brother."

Nicole had no reason to think she would be a part of that meeting. Gavin was a grown man. He didn't need her holding his hand. Even so, this situation escalated every day. "It feels strange now—having people know when he hasn't met anyone yet."

"We're preparing his family, that's all. Family who will love him, welcome him."

She looked at the packet in her hand. Was this the right move? Her surety of the situation threatened to crumble at the reality of the papers. Selling the Victorian made perfect sense, though. She didn't want to live here. She and Gavin had a home in Lincoln Park.

But he didn't have a permanent job. Not since the crash.

She was his only true anchor to Lincoln Park. That thought sent a chill through her veins. "I understand. But he knows nothing of you or your family. He doesn't know there are people waiting to welcome him. He just knows that I lied to him his whole life."

"And he thinks I didn't want anything to do with him."

Nicole wondered at the wisdom of letting Gavin process all this on his own. "Maybe we should intervene."

"With a promise to leave him alone after he has all the facts. Give him time to think."

Nicole set the packet on the hood of Rowdy Red. "I don't know the right decision. I really don't. The more I think about him trying to sort this out without my full explanation of what really happened, the more it doesn't seem right."

"We know where he is, Nicole."

Adam took a few steps toward her but stopped a respectable distance away. Her breath hitched at the thought of being in his arms again, a scenario she knew wouldn't happen. But what if it *did*?

Nothing romantic could come out of her and Adam joining forces to help Gavin. They were teaming up for the good of their son, nothing more. The faster she signed the contract, the faster she could say good-bye to Hawks Valley. The emotional toll of Gavin showing up unexpectedly—and finding out about Adam the way he did—couldn't detour her original plans.

The plans she knew made the most sense and were best for everyone. "I'll text him. Tell him we would like to talk to him."

Adam followed her into the house, grabbing her coffee cup while she carried the weight of the contract. She picked up her phone, took a deep breath and texted Gavin.

"Now we wait, I guess." She shoved her phone in her pocket after making sure that the notifications were turned on.

"Do you want some help? I saw the garage open. It might make the time pass quicker. Mom took Kylie to a friend's birthday party."

"No flights today?" she asked.

"Nope. The big wedding is today. Tomorrow afternoon is full, though, with everyone leaving."

Nicole debated about letting Adam help her. It's not like cleaning tools, nuts and bolts out of a garage would lead to a bonding experience. "Okay. I'll grab us a couple of waters."

An hour passed as the dump pile increased. "Only two more boxes on the shelves. Thank you, Adam. We've made great progress."

He pulled down the remaining boxes and opened the first one. He sat across from her, the folding chairs she had found in the first closet coming in handy. "It's interesting the things people save."

"Yep. Simply to be thrown out years later. But this isn't tools or gardening stuff." Confused, she pulled out a couple of books and laughed. "My elementary school yearbooks." They spent the next few minutes flipping through them, first finding their pictures, then looking at everyone else's. They commented on the changes in styles regarding clothing and hair, who was still here in town and who had moved away.

"I wonder why my dad saved all these." She dug through the box, pulling out more yearbooks including her high school ones. "I don't even want to look at those." She set them on the cement floor.

"That's why the box was so heavy."

"What's this?" Nicole pulled out the last item in the box. It was wrapped in brown packing paper. She unwrapped it and gasped. "Oh, look, a picture." Tears pooled in her eyes.

"What?" Adam asked. "What kind of picture?"

She stared at the double framed photo. On the left side was a picture of her on the swing when she was about three years old. The photo on the right side featured Gavin, on the same swing, when he was three as well, that quick visit they made here the year before her father passed away. How did she not know about this picture? She handed the photo to Adam, thankful she could show it to him.

"I can't believe this was stuck in the bottom of the box. Look… I'm on the left and Gavin is on the right. I guess my dad took this picture of him. I've never seen this before, though. He must have had it framed after I left. Weird that this box was hidden amongst all the tools."

"Gavin was in Hawks Valley?"

The tone of Adam's voice instantly put her on guard. Her heart pounded. "Once. Just for a weekend."

"Incredible." His hurt spewed out in his flat, crisp response.

All her sentimental emotions vanished as she tried to find an adequate explanation. "I didn't know what to do, Adam. You were married. For almost five years at that point."

He pushed back on the chair. "I'm trying to understand, Nicole."

"When I brought Gavin here, it did make me think. Made me wonder what he might be missing. Then when Dad passed away, I decided to tell you when I came down for the funeral. I just knew you'd be there and I had planned on setting up a time to meet with you. But you never showed. Then I found out you weren't in town the whole week I packed up the house."

Adam stood, shoving his hands in his pockets. "That was a blip in the twenty-four years. A *blip*."

"Like I told your mom, it seemed every time I went to tell you, God shut a door."

"I know, then you locked it."

"But I didn't throw away the key. We're having this conversation, aren't we?"

He stood and started to pace. "What else haven't you told me? I feel like every time I'm somewhat settled, I'm thrown another secret you've kept from me. This time it was a visit."

Nicole's phone dinged, saving her from an immediate response. "It's Gavin."

Her hand actually shook. His response was only a swipe away. She opened the text.

Hitching in a breath, Adam rested his hands on the back of the folding chair. "What did he say?"

Nicole stood. "Let's go."

They rode silently to the lodge even though Adam had a million more questions to ask Nicole. He'd almost skirted around her wishes earlier this morning while he replaced his mom's car battery in the Woodvale parking lot. But common sense prevailed. He had told Nicole they were in this together, so he stood by his word.

Now here they were. Together. He parked the car. "Now what?" Knowing he would meet his son in a matter of minutes gave the words a sudden urgency.

"He's staying in one of the cabins." She looked at her phone. "Eight. Bear Trail."

He came around and opened her door. "I'm not sure I'm ready for this."

"Do you want to stay here while I go talk to him?"

Those words sent his stomach into a spiral. "No. I'm in. To be honest, I'm nervous. Very nervous."

They started walking, following the signs to the cabin area and Bear Trail. She gave him a shy smile. "I'm glad you're being honest. That's what we all need to be."

He didn't mention that she hadn't been honest over the last two decades. But regardless, he vowed to keep Nicole's dishonesty front and center whenever his mind drifted to her. In moments, he would meet his son who would be a part of his future. At least he prayed so. There were no manuals on how to meet a son you never knew you had. No training. At least he had a few minutes' warning.

He wasn't sure he could count that as a good thing,

though. But maybe the element of surprise had a benefit. Like not having your stomach wound up in knots.

They turned down Bear Trail, their footsteps echoing their silence on the beaten down pine-straw path, wide enough for walkers and a golf cart. The sun filtered through the trees, keeping the noontime temperature down.

As they passed cabin six, he noticed Nicole's steps slowing. He grabbed her hand, instinctively needing to comfort her. She didn't let go. Her hand in his felt natural. Right.

Like they belonged together. Which they did. But only for this time. Only regarding their son. Adam couldn't lose sight of Nicole's quarter of a century deception.

He followed her up the narrow porch steps and stood behind her as she put her hand to the door to knock. Before her knuckles touched the dark wood the door swung open. Adam's throat tightened as he stared into his son's eyes for the very first time, blinking back tears as Gavin's eyes widened as well.

Nicole stood between them, the real-life metaphor of the last twenty-four years.

In two steps she embraced Gavin, Adam watching as his son hugged Nicole. "Ma."

She stepped back, then to the side. "Gavin. This is Adam Hawk."

Adam held out his hand, his heart close to bursting. "Hi." He didn't know what else to say, not that any more words would have come out. Gavin took his hand, a strong handshake following. He would count that as a start.

"Come on in."

Adam followed Nicole into the cabin, but couldn't take his eyes off his son, who sat on the couch, motioning Nicole to sit beside him. Adam took a seat in the oversize armchair next to the couch. If he were in any other situation, he'd be appreciating the excellence of the Woodvale cabin and its furnishings, but his attention solely stayed on Gavin.

"Thank you for seeing us." Nicole looked from Gavin to Adam, then back. "We wanted to talk to you together. Clear up some issues. Then if you still need time, we'll respect that."

"Are you guys a couple now?" Gavin's gaze darted from Nicole to Adam.

Just when Adam thought his gut couldn't be punched harder, that question almost went right through him.

"No!" Nicole blurted.

"Just wondering." Gavin looked at Adam. "I saw you guys holding hands coming down the path."

How did he explain that they were holding on for dear life?

"That was for support, Gavin. That's all." Nicole's voice sounded surprisingly calm and steady, something Adam wasn't sure he could pull off right now.

"Gavin, I wanted to set you straight about Adam. As I tried to explain before, he didn't know about you until I came to Hawks Valley last week. He was as surprised as you were."

The young man stood, moving around to brace his hands on the back of the sister chair of the one Adam sat in. "I don't understand, Ma. Why all the secrecy? The lies?"

"I know I owe you an explanation. Decisions made when you're young and scared aren't always the wisest. Adam had become engaged to another woman, his father had just passed away from—"

"Your mom came to town to tell me, but felt I wasn't

in a place to be receptive. We'll never know whether her assessment was right, because again, at such a young age, I have no idea how I would have reacted. But—" Adam stood, wanting to be eye level with his son "—we can rehash the past or we can think of the here and now. I did just find out about you, and right here and now, I want to know you. I hear we have a lot in common."

Adam purposefully cut off Nicole before she told Gavin about the crash. Again, without a training manual, he had no idea if he did the right thing, but keeping the conversation on the three of them seemed paramount to him. There'd be plenty of time to tell Gavin about his grandfather and the real reason for Nicole's revelation.

"I see that, too," Gavin admitted. "I've been doing some research. You're a pretty good pilot. Even gotten out of a few scrapes."

A humbled Adam tried to process that his son had been interested enough to find out some information about him. "A couple, I guess. I love my job."

Gavin's gaze lowered. "Your wife passed away. I'm sorry."

Another gut punch. "Thank you." He must know about Kylie. "I have a daughter who is very excited to meet you. When you're ready of course."

Nicole stood. "Why don't I let you two talk?"

"No, Ma. Stay. I want you to stay." He walked over and they both sat. "There are so many things I want to know. I don't know where to start."

Adam sat back down, gratefulness filling his heart, which still threatened to burst at any moment. His son.

In the next hour, Nicole retold Gavin the story she'd told Adam. Expectation, anticipation, regret, certainty, curiosity. All those emotions ran through Adam as he listened to Nicole spill her heart to her son.

"I promise I only thought of you and what was best for you at the time. Like I said, I was much too young to be making such bold decisions. But I had to."

Gavin looked straight at Adam. "I'd like to meet your daughter sometime."

"You let me know when. I can arrange it. Her name is Kylie and she's a joy. She's six and full of life. Her favorite thing is dancing. She takes lessons here at Woodvale."

"She doesn't like to read," Nicole offered. "Like someone else I remember."

Gavin's glance shifted between Adam and Nicole. "Are you sure you're not a couple? Sounds like you're pretty involved, Ma."

"We're not."

"Why aren't you a couple?"

Now Adam's gut shredded. Apparently no question was off the table for Gavin. Adam guessed he couldn't blame him. Twenty-four years of secrecy spun a whole lot of ideas, questions and scenarios.

"Gavin, I'm here to sell the house and get back to Lincoln Park. Adam has a life here. We haven't seen each other in years, and we've moved on."

And just like that Nicole snuffed out any possibility of a future with him. Her words were probably best spoken now, and they solidified what Adam knew. Like she said, they had both moved on.

"Then why all this?" Gavin motioned his arm between the three of them. "You just decided, 'Hey, my kid is twenty-four. Let me tell him about his dad. Oh, and I'll tell his dad about him. Then I'll leave town.' That doesn't make sense to me, Ma."

Would Nicole keep to her promise of honesty? Would she tell Gavin the reason she decided to reveal all? He watched as she closed her eyes for a few seconds.

"I thought Adam could help you." Her words came out whispered, tentative and unsure all at once.

"Help me with what?"

"Flying." Adam stood. "Your mom knows how important flying is to you. She wants to see you back in the air, pursuing your passion."

"Ha." Gavin pointed to Nicole. "She would be the happiest person in the world if I never flew a plane again."

Nicole uncrossed her arms and clasped her hands. "That was the truth at one time, but now, I want to see you happy. And if flying makes you happy, and I know it does, then that's what you should do."

The air, thick with revelation, surrounded them. Gavin looked at Nicole, disbelief written all over his face. "Are you being for real?"

Adam nodded. "She's for real, Gavin. What else would have caused her to shake up so many lives, for the better I might add, but shake them up nonetheless?"

Gavin's gaze intensified toward Nicole. "So, all this wasn't really about meeting my dad? It was about pulling me out of a supposed funk you think I'm in?"

Adam blew out a breath as tension shattered the progress made over the last couple of hours. "She cares about you, Gavin, more than she cares about anyone in the world."

Gavin, shifting his gaze to Adam, ran a hand through his thick, unruly hair. "So why are you really here? Self-help guru or dad?"

"Gavin!" Nicole sat straighter on the couch.

"It's okay, Nicole." Adam carefully counted to ten before speaking to Gavin. "I want to be in your life. As a father. If I can be of help in other ways, that's a bonus."

Gavin shook his head. "It's weird knowing all of a sudden that you have a dad. Like I've gotten along without one all these years, why would I need one now?"

Adam tried to stay confident, despite his son's out-loud musings. "Who says you need one? But you have one. Might as well take advantage of that where you can. Besides, you are also a big brother. It's give and take any way you look at it."

Gavin tried to hide a half smile, but it didn't escape Adam. He pulled out his phone. "Nicole sent us each other's numbers. We can keep in touch. You can let me know when you're ready to meet Kylie. I can even send you a few photos."

Gavin picked up his phone from the table. "She did, but I deleted it."

Adam's heart sunk.

"But send me your number." Gavin held up his phone.

Adam held his breath as he sent a text to Gavin that said "hi."

A request for a phone number signaled a start.

Chapter Eight

Adam looked at his phone for the hundredth time since arriving at church. Nothing. No text or missed call from Gavin. He said his hellos and chatted with a couple of friends before retrieving Kylie from her Sunday school class.

"Here you go, Kylie." Blair, the teenage teacher, gave his daughter a paper that she had colored.

"Thanks, Blair. Kylie always loves coming to Sunday school." Adam held one of Kylie's hands as her other one fisted the paper.

"Bye, Miss Blair." Kylie waved, the paper fluttering.

"Bye. See you next week."

The two of them made their way to the car. Adam, still dazed from yesterday's meeting with Gavin, functioned on autopilot today. He couldn't remember the sermon message. He couldn't remember what hymns they sang.

Life right now resembled a blur. He needed to straighten up before his flights today. After lunch, he dropped Kylie at his mom's. She'd been bothering him about the details from yesterday, but he begged for time. Gracious as always, Shelley agreed.

Riles greeted him when he entered the hangar. "Hawk has arrived."

"Don't you ever take a day off, old man?" Adam asked.

Riles smiled, not offended by the greeting. "I'll take a day when you take a day. This place is going to be busy with that fancy wedding being over."

"I've got back-to-back flights. Not long ones, though."

"That's why I'm here. You okay?"

"Yep." Adam had checked the computer in the office area, making sure nothing had changed for today. He glanced at his phone. "My group should be arriving soon. Is the logbook ready to sign off on?"

"It is. All pre-flight checks are completed. You sure you don't want to talk?" Riles raised an eyebrow.

"I'm sure." His mentor would be a great sounding board, but Adam didn't have time to tell the whole story right now. Adam couldn't wait for Gavin and Riles to meet. Riles had always been a mentor to Adam, and he couldn't imagine Riles being anything less for Gavin.

Adam knew he didn't have all the answers, but he'd like a shot at being a father to his son.

"You met the boy?" Riles sat at the table, a new puzzle started. He pushed pieces around, not interlocking any of them.

"I did."

"And?"

"He's a good man." Adam shrugged. "He just needs time."

"And you?"

Their words bounced back and forth like a ping-pong ball. "I just want to know him."

Adam reflected back to lunch with Kylie as she told him about the Sunday school lesson with the boy who came home after being gone a long time. *The daddy still loved him,* she said. *Just like God would always love us.*

Gavin was no prodigal, but Adam related to welcoming a son home and the love that went along with it. Adam loved Gavin. He wanted to be a father to him. He longed to embrace him in a hug and have that embrace returned.

"All in good time," Riles said. "The good Lord has impeccable timing."

Adam's phone dinged with a text. "Wren has arrived with a guest."

He texted that he was in the hangar, and he'd meet them in a minute. Wren often drove the shuttle that brought the guests to the airport from the lodge. Wren, Lark's sister, had graduated a couple of years before Adam. She'd married and left Woodvale and Hawks Valley for a while until her husband died. She returned last year with her son, Ethan, to heal from her husband's death. Woodvale needed a front desk manager, and Wren stepped into the role. Wren and Lark, although sisters, were complete opposites.

Adam stood.

Riles followed. "Oops. I'm supposed to be in the terminal greetin' folks."

Adam turned. "It's a bit early. Flight doesn't leave here for over an hour."

"Some folks get a little nervous about flight times."

The two of them walked into the terminal area.

Turned out there was only one guest.

Gavin.

"I'll pick you up in a little while when I drop off the other guests. Bye, guys." Wren waved before walking out the door.

"Bye, Wren." Adam pivoted. "Hi, Gavin." Adam stood,

still unaccustomed to seeing a reminder of himself in his younger years.

"Hi." Gavin glanced over at Riles who stood next to Adam.

"Hello, there. I'm Riles. Pilot, greeter, mechanic and cleanup crew for this place. You must be Gavin."

Gavin's gaze flitted between Riles and Adam.

"Riles is a good man, Gavin. A good friend."

His son nodded. "Thought I'd take a look around if that's okay."

"Sure." Adam threw a prayer of thanks up to God that he had a few minutes to show Gavin the place that kept him sane. "I can give you a quick tour if you'd like."

"Okay."

Gavin didn't say much as they toured the facility. Adam's mind raced at what this meant—that the young man just showed up here without warning. Did he expect Adam to be here? Was he surprised?

The moments seemed surreal. *Was this really happening?* Questions stacked one on top of each other in Adam's mind as they walked around. But he'd file them away for later. Right now he didn't want to ask questions. Questions might turn Gavin away. He decided to take the slow approach. Good Lord willing, he'd have plenty of years to learn everything about his son. The fact that he showed up at the airport had to be a good sign regarding his love of flying. They reached the hangar and Adam ushered him inside.

"Who's the puzzle guy? You?" Gavin nodded toward the table where Riles had his current puzzle spread out.

"No. That's Riles. He loves a good jigsaw puzzle."

"Me, too." Gavin walked over, studying the pieces as he stood over the table. Moments later he picked up a piece and placed it in a spot toward the top border. "He's not gonna be mad that I placed that piece, is he?"

Adam watched as Gavin scooted another piece around. "No. A lot of people walk by and place a piece or two."

"Too bad life isn't more like a puzzle. There are a lot of pieces in real life that don't fit anywhere." Gavin tapped another piece into place.

Adam didn't know what to say to that. He didn't want to be glib or cheesy. But he did want to be honest. "Most pieces fit somewhere, though. That's the good news. Come here, I want to show you something."

They walked to the back of the hangar. Gavin's eyes widened when he saw Adam's plane. "That's a cool ride." He reached up to touch the sleek, shiny side.

"Yeah, she's a beauty. She rides nice, too. I'd love to take you up sometime."

Gavin instantly retracted his hand and shoved it in his pocket. "I need to get back. That woman from Woodvale should be here with your group. She's giving me a lift back to the lodge."

The tension of his son not acknowledging his offer hung thick in the air. But at least the offer had been given. And Adam wouldn't trade anything for these few minutes he had with Gavin, who didn't say many words. But Adam watched him take in everything.

A quick good-bye with a handshake and a thank you had Gavin walking out the door as the group came in. A short while later, everyone had settled in the plane, including Adam.

He taxied the plane to the runway, his mind focused on the flight ahead. Progress. He and Gavin had made progress. Maybe he would want to meet Kylie soon. And Adam's mom. As rough as she was on Nicole after learning the truth, she couldn't wait to meet her grandson.

* * *

Nicole stared at the contract still sitting on her kitchen table. A blue pen, not nearly as fancy as Mary's, sat next to the stack of papers. Her phone said eight o'clock. Too late to call the realtor tonight.

Nicole had read every word carefully. Nothing sounded out of the ordinary. Like Mary said, standard contract. So why couldn't she bring herself to sign?

She didn't hear from Gavin today, even though she'd sent him a text. She didn't want to barge in on him at Woodvale, so she'd spent the day working on the last closet in the garage. The framed photo of her and Gavin sat on the dresser in her room.

Her phone dinged with a text. Adam wanting to know if he could drop by.

She texted him yes.

He knocked on her door less than a half hour later, carrying a bag with two take-out containers. "Not sure if you ate or not, but I didn't, so I brought enough for two."

Motioning him in, she wondered if she would miss Adam's spontaneous visits. She eyed the still unsigned papers, then shifted her gaze to the dark-haired man who had the ability to cause her to rethink her decisions.

Shaking off her dangerous thoughts they settled at the table, the containers opened, each of them eating the pulled pork, mac and cheese and green beans with the plastic cutlery provided.

"So may I ask why you wanted to come by and bring me dinner?" Nicole set her fork down and grabbed her water.

"Gavin came to the airport today."

She stood. *"What?* Why didn't you call me? What happened? Does he want to fly?"

"Whoa. This is why I didn't call you. Besides, I had

two flights. Sit down and I'll tell you about the visit." He sighed. "Is Gavin usually a man of few words? Or is it just being around me?"

"Depends." Nicole's hands brushed nervously over the top of the chair.

"Wren brought him over in the shuttle. He met Riles, then I showed him around. We went to the hangar area last. When I offered to take him up in my plane sometime, he got squirrelly and said he needed to go." He pinned her with his blue gaze. "It's progress, Nicole. I'm hoping he'll want to meet Kylie and Mom soon."

She sat, her appetite not as robust as it was five minutes ago. "I texted him today but never heard back."

"One step at a time."

"Easy for you to say, as you were the first step." Nicole picked up the fork and started pushing food around.

"We can't navigate these waters for him. He's an adult." Adam continued eating.

"But he's still my baby." A mother's heart always wanted to help her child. Age didn't matter.

Adam nodded to the papers Nicole had pushed aside when they opened the takeout. "Mary hasn't come by to pick those up yet?"

Nicole shrugged. "I haven't signed them."

"Have you changed your mind about selling?" He tore off a piece of the toasted bread with a look she couldn't quite discern on his face.

Did she detect a hint of hopefulness? "No."

She knew her voice sounded iffy, and she needed to explain. "It's the only thing that makes sense. But when Mary has the contract in hand, then people will start showing up and that's what I'm not ready for. I needed to give my brain a couple of days to settle down from our meeting with Gavin."

"Oh, okay."

Adam certainly seemed okay with her plans. Why wouldn't he be? He now had his in with Gavin. Which meant he had no other reason to delay the sale.

Although she had to admit that after yesterday's meeting, having them all three together had been a dream come true. A fantasy of hers since she found out she carried Adam's child. Her wildest yearnings never had the situation playing out twenty plus years later, but, regardless, it finally happened.

The two men she loved in one room.

Wait? *Loved?*

Well, that word could be referring to the present, but also the past. She currently loved Gavin, and previously loved Adam.

Right?

But now, looking at him as he sat across from her— his strong features only more handsome with age, his dark black hair tinged with the slightest of gray and his composure cool and collected as they talked about their son—could have her falling for him all over again.

Unless she'd never unfallen from all those years ago.

The past mingled with the present. Each separate, yet so alike in many ways. How easy would it be to keep the house, move back to Hawks Valley and be a part of this community once again?

Adam licked the barbecue sauce off his fork before setting it down. "Even though Gavin didn't say a whole lot today, I felt we connected. I'm looking forward to more time alone with him. If he wants to be a part of our lives, once you're back in Lincoln Park, we can have good quality time without distractions. Just getting to know the Hawks, his sister."

Her heart lurched. She now knew that she totally misread him a few moments ago. He couldn't wait for her to leave so he could hone in on Gavin. No wonder he asked about the contract. Nicole had no desire to stay where she wasn't wanted. She had already been there and done that.

Yes, Adam gave her Gavin, the best gift ever, but she wouldn't be played again by this man. She grabbed the papers and the pen, blinking back tears as she stood quickly and turned her back to him. Any thoughts on rekindling a relationship with Adam would only set her up for another heart shattered like glass.

Her resolve helped dry her tears as she quickly signed everywhere the yellow sticky arrows indicated. When she finished, she picked up her phone to text Mary that the contract had been signed.

She held up the phone, pivoting to find Adam shoving the take-out boxes into the plastic bag they arrived in, oblivious to the chaos in her heart and mind. "There you go. Mary is picking up the contract first thing in the morning. I'll be out of your way and hair as soon as I can."

Adam stopped tying the bag handles together, a dumbfounded look on his face. "What?"

She slid the papers on the table. "You and Gavin need time together. I understand."

"Okay." He set the bag on the table. "Is there something else you want to say?"

Nicole couldn't imagine putting words to her feelings right now. The hopes, the lost dreams, the many nights wondering what life would have been like if she ended up with Adam, and if she, Gavin and Adam had been a family from the beginning. She had envisioned it happening as many ways as there were stars in the sky.

And it never had.

"I want what is best for Gavin. And if that's him getting to know you without me being in the way, that's what has to happen. I'll do—"

"Anything for your son. I know. I would, too."

She knew he had no idea how often he used to finish her sentences in high school when they were truly the best of friends. She crushed on him, but even after he eventually started dating Rebecca, Nicole had always held out hope he'd see that she was the one for him. Twenty-five years later and it hadn't happened yet.

And now she knew she had to give up. Surrender. Wave the white flag of regret.

But she would never regret having Gavin. No one could take him away from her. No one. But what about a town? Could the promise of family and her welcoming hometown lure her son away from their life in the city? The life they'd built, just the two of them?

If Nicole were a praying girl, she'd toss that one up to God for sure. But she wasn't. Hadn't been in a long time. What God would leave all her prayers unanswered? Apparently He answered some prayers. She saw her old community church parking lot full when she went out for coffee this morning at the diner.

There might have been a small tug, but Nicole quickly brushed that away as nostalgia. .

Tonight had reinforced that opinion even more. No, Nicole had a great life in Lincoln Park. She loved her teaching career, and she had friends and favorite places to eat. She'd moved on from childish and teenage dreams quite nicely. And had raised an amazing young man by herself.

Standing on her own had taken her this far, and she didn't need anyone else to help her usher in the future. Especially Adam Hawk.

Chapter Nine

Adam nervously paced the floor of his house. Not even the beautiful, serene view of the river and mountains he saw out of his wall of windows could settle him. In just a few minutes, Gavin would be here to meet Kylie and his grandma.

Kylie had put on her prettiest dress. Adam's mom had baked her lemon pound cake. They'd already eaten dinner, Adam not wanting to compound the meeting with a meal. That could turn awkward.

No, best to keep it simple. Coffee and dessert. If Gavin even drank coffee. There were so many things Adam wanted to learn about his son.

"Daddy? Do I look pretty?" Kylie twirled around the living room, her blue-and-yellow, flowery dress floating as she spun.

"You always look pretty." Even through hints of Rebecca's features, the Hawk DNA ran strong in Kylie. She and Gavin both boasted Adam's dark hair and blue eyes. Gavin stood taller than his father, but not by much.

"Adam, honey. I'm here." Shelley came through the front door, and Adam grabbed the cake platter she held. "One lemon pound cake at your service."

He set the platter on the granite counter of the bar area in the kitchen. "Thanks, Mom. I've started the coffee brewing. It's strange not knowing whether Gavin likes coffee or lemon pound cake."

"He's not a Hawk if he doesn't like lemon pound cake, or a pilot if he doesn't like coffee. Am I right?" Shelley smiled, but Adam sensed her nervousness.

Her words, probably meant to lighten the mood, struck Adam hard. "He is a Hawk, Mom. And he always will be."

"I know, honey. I'm just talking too much. That happens when I'm nervous. You know that."

The doorbell rang. Adam realized his palms were sweaty as he reached to open the front door. Gavin stood holding a bouquet of flowers.

"Come on in," Adam said, shutting the door after his son walked in. Within seconds, Kylie had her arms wrapped around Adam's leg. She stared up at Gavin, wonder in her gaze and a timid smile on her face.

"Gavin, this is Kylie."

"Hi," Kylie said, her right foot wrapping around Adam's leg. He hoped she'd stop being shy momentarily.

"Hello. These are for you." Gavin held out the flowers.

"For me?" Kylie unwrapped herself from Adam and grabbed the bouquet of purple, red, yellow and orange flowers. "These are pretty."

"What else do you say, Kylie?" Adam asked.

"Thank you." She sniffed the flowers. "They smell pretty, too."

"Why, those are mighty gorgeous flowers." Shelley walked in from the kitchen, a tissue clutched in her fist. Tears welled as she looked at Gavin. "You must be Gavin. I'm Shelley Hawk, Adam's mother. Your grandmother." Her words started out strong, yet ended in a whisper.

Gavin stared at Shelley a moment. "It's nice to meet you. I thought you might like some chocolates." He handed her a small box. "Ma says all ladies like chocolate."

Shelley dabbed at her eyes. "Your mom would be right. Thank you. Wow...they look fancy. I'm sure they're delicious. Adam, do you have a vase for Kylie's flowers?"

"Under the sink, I think. Let's go into the living room." Adam led the way while Shelley slipped into the kitchen.

"This is a great house." Gavin stood in front of the windows. "Nice view."

"This property had been in the family for years. I bought it outright and built this house almost twenty years ago." Adam stood by Gavin, cherishing these few moments alone with him while the girls arranged the flowers in a vase.

"I was four."

Adam wondered if their relationship would be a forever tug of what could have been versus what was. He hoped not. He certainly wanted to know about Gavin's childhood and life up to this point, but also needed to concentrate on moving forward, building a current relationship. More than anything, he wanted Gavin to be a part of the Hawk family and all their traditions.

"Your flowers look pretty in the vase, Gabin."

Adam and Gavin turned at the sound of Kylie's voice.

"It's Gavin, princess. With a 'V,'" Adam said.

"It's cool." Gavin gave Kylie a high five. "Kind of cute."

Everyone settled on the couch and love seat. Adam quickly realized the situation as becoming awkward. Like an inquisition would be starting soon. "How about we go outside? It's a cool evening and we can show Gavin your swing set and playhouse."

"Yay. Let's do that." Kylie stood and led the way through the kitchen to the sliding doors that led outside.

"You go on," Shelley said. "I'm going to grab a plastic tablecloth and set up outside for the dessert. Go on." She shooed Adam as he hesitated.

He smiled at everyone being themselves. Natural. Not perched on the edge of a sofa, waiting for one-word, polite answers to the top ten questions you ask a man when you find out he's your son.

Or grandson.

Or half brother.

Kylie had wiggled her way onto the swing by the time Adam made it outside. Gavin stood behind her, ready to push.

Adam thought back to the picture Nicole had discovered in the garage. Gavin as a young boy sitting on a swing. A pang of regret ran through Adam, but he refused to give in to it and decided instead to live in this full circle moment God had given him.

"I live right by a park that has swings like this. I used to swing all the time," Gavin volunteered as he gave Kylie the first push.

"Did you go high in the sky?"

"I did."

Small talk ensued over the next few minutes as Kylie went from swinging to sliding to climbing up the ladder and hiding in her playhouse. Tidbits of Gavin's life came out. Nothing earth shattering, just ordinary life. He had fallen off a slide one time, needing stitches in his elbow. And had a friend who would always bring their dog to the park with them. He told Kylie a couple of funny kid jokes.

Adam's heart swelled at the way God blessed them that evening. The future couldn't be predicted, not every night could be guaranteed to be like this, but for tonight, Adam couldn't be more grateful.

"Who wants dessert?" Shelley stood on the patio, the table set for four.

"We all do." Adam nodded toward the table. "Let's sit."

"So, do you prefer coffee? Iced tea? Something else?" Shelley asked her grandson.

"I'm a coffee guy." Gavin slid into the chair across from Adam as Kylie squirmed into the chair to his left.

"Grandma's cake is the bestest in the world." Kylie rested her elbows on the table, clutching her fork in one hand.

Gavin picked up his fork, a grin gracing his face. "I can't wait to try it."

Shelley dished out slices, then passed them around.

"Very good." Gavin closed his eyes for a moment after taking the first bite. "I think you're right about it being the bestest." He turned to Shelley. "This is delicious."

Shelley winked at Adam. "Told you."

Adam wondered where this would lead. Would Gavin come and visit a couple times a year? Would he be a part of their holidays? Would he let them celebrate his birthday with him?

Would Nicole be a part of all these times? He could picture her here. His heart saddened at the knowledge she didn't want to be in Hawks Valley. They'd always been best friends in school. Then the month they dated, he'd started seeing her in a new way. But Rebecca had beckoned him back to the life he'd known all through high school and he ran back, scared at what would happen if he didn't.

Now Adam played the game of what could have been in his mind. He didn't entertain those thoughts very long, though. No scenario would stop him from wanting Kylie in his life. He cherished his daughter.

But Nicole had come back, and all those best friend

qualities were still there. Turmoil still ensued when he thought about how she kept his son from him all this time, but again, Gavin sat here now. On this patio. With his half sister and his grandma.

Go forward. Stop looking back.

Peering at Gavin, Adam realized he was thankful Nicole brought Gavin to Hawks Valley. He was thankful she raised a good young man. But as thankful as he was, that was as far as he could go with her. He obviously wasn't good at reading women. She'd kept a secret from him for over twenty years, and Rebecca had been so unhappy that she wanted a divorce while he thought they were fine. No, he and women were better off as friends

And as a friendly gesture, maybe he'd invite her to his mom's surprise birthday party. All of Shelley's loved ones would be there. He'd invite Gavin, too, of course. Then an idea came to him. Nicole could help make his mom a photo album like she'd made for him about Gavin. He'd enlist her help like he would enlist any of his friends' help.

That thought not only relieved undue pressure in finding the perfect gift for his mom, it also would prove he could work with Nicole without becoming involved.

"Adam. Are you with us?"

Shelley's voice interrupted his birthday planning. "Uh, yes. Just lost in a thought."

"Do you want another slice of cake?"

"No, thank you."

Gavin looked at his sister. "I can imagine you have fun growing up in this house. Along this river."

Kylie nodded. "It is fun. I like living here."

"Maybe someday you can come and see where I grew up? It's not too late to turn you into a city girl."

"What's a city girl?" Kylie asked.

Gavin gently tugged one of her pigtails. "It's just a girl who lives in the city."

Kylie giggled, then Gavin switched his focus to Adam. "I called Ma. I checked out of Woodvale. I'm going to stay with her and help her with the house. She's done most of the clearing out. Now she says there's just cleaning. Mops and brooms cleaning, I guess. There are two showings coming up. She's anxious to be done and back home, she said."

Adam became on edge. Gavin and Nicole still lived in Lincoln Park. The thought of them leaving, let alone so soon, grounded him in the reality of the situation.

None of this was permanent.

Maybe he could ask Gavin to stay in Hawks Valley when Nicole went back. But why did the thought of Nicole leaving bother him?

Gavin, he understood. Nicole? Not so much.

She'd made a bold statement when she didn't tell him about his son. Nothing says "We aren't going to be together" more than keeping their son a secret for twenty-four years. It might be best if Nicole did return to Lincoln Park.

"I'm not sure, Adam." Nicole looked at the two boxes he had set on her kitchen floor and the brand-new scrapbook album he held in his hand.

"What's not to be sure about? You did a great job with Gavin's book."

Adam looked too attractive to refuse anything, but she just might refuse this. Asking her to help him build a photo album of his mom's life for her birthday had a personal aspect that Nicole found daunting. "I can't have boxes and stuff sitting around. Mary is going to be showing the house."

Adam set the album on the table. "That's a lame excuse. There are plenty of places to store all of this out of sight."

"I think you should do it, Ma."

Nicole turned to find Gavin standing in the doorway. "We still have things to do here, Gavin."

Her son shrugged. "It's not that much. I wouldn't mind looking at some of the pictures Adam brought over."

Gavin still hadn't called Adam Dad, and no one expected him to. These new relationships were still in the building process and who knew at what point something might come along to stall or stop the progress.

"Maybe if we all worked on it together," Nicole said, as she sat at the table, still not sure about this endeavor. It seemed even more personal now that Gavin had joined in. They had just separated several piles of pictures when Gavin looked at his watch, then stood.

"I have to go. I told Kylie I would watch her dance class today."

"Thanks for your help." Adam nodded toward the table.

"Well, bye." Nicole turned and watched as Gavin left.

Maybe it was for the best, though. These pictures were bringing back all kinds of memories. Some good, some wishful.

Some painful.

She'd been a part of Adam's life since childhood, but never totally in. Always one step removed, and Nicole didn't see that changing. Now, Gavin had one foot in, it seemed. Going to watch Kylie's dance class?

She tried not to escalate the situation to more than what it was. Gavin had chosen to check out of Woodvale and stay with her at the Victorian. As long as he had one foot with her and one with the Hawks, she wouldn't spiral.

She hoped.

"Has Gavin said anything more about coming to the airport again?" Nicole threw a blurry picture into the box designated for pictures not being used in the album.

"No." Adam held up a picture of himself standing next to a plane. "Look. Maybe we could pull the picture of Gavin standing next to the plane out of the album you made me and put it in Mom's."

Nicole's chest tightened. "What?"

Adam smiled. "I thought it would be cool if we added some pictures from my album."

"Your album?" Nicole's mind spun. The album she poured her heart and soul into would suddenly be a part of a birthday present for Shelley Hawk?

"You made it for me, right? I'd just like to use some of the photos. They're all I have, remember?"

"I need a minute." Nicole walked outside, trying to clear her mind. Gray skies matched her mood. Leaves rustled overhead, their branches swaying. The swing moved back and forth in a slow dance, the wind its guide. Before sitting she looked toward the house and she saw Adam still at the table, head down. She had no idea what she expected when she revealed Gavin's existence, but it wasn't that her heart would be pulled in two directions. Yes, Gavin needed to know Adam and the rest of the family. But she wanted to keep him to herself as well. Like they'd been the last twenty-four years. Just the two of them. She knew her musings presented an impossible situation.

If Gavin hadn't been in the crash, would she be sitting with Adam today? In the Victorian, with Gavin at his half sisters' dance class? Or would she be in Lincoln Park, enjoying her summer break, renting the Victorian to a new family.

New family.

That's what Gavin had now. A new family that didn't include her. Nicole thought about the spread of pictures on the table. She'd been a part of that once. In thinking of Adam, she'd been so close to being so much more than a friend, for a few weeks anyway.

And now she wanted to leave. The sooner the better. She and Gavin probably had a few hours worth of cleaning up to do. Mary could overnight any contracts to sign.

Yes, that would be best.

But Gavin hadn't made any strides in being ready to fly. Maybe he'd find new life here in Hawks Valley, but nothing made him happier than flying.

"Hey, penny for your thoughts."

Adam walked out into the yard, stopping a few feet away from the swing. Her toes mingled with the patchy grass springing up from the worn earth, anchoring her to a stop. Looking at Adam never became old. His good looks rocked of course, but his whole presence, confidence, spoke volumes.

She couldn't let him interfere with her life. He wasn't forever. He wasn't even temporary. Adam was the father of her son, period. She pushed disappointment away, focusing on reality. "Not sure what my thoughts are, so I don't want to rip you off. Save your penny for someone else."

"Nicole. This doesn't have to be difficult. I'm asking for your help in an area you excel in. My mom will be forever grateful. And adding pictures of Gavin is only fitting."

Nicole nudged the dirt with her toe. What could helping Adam hurt? She'd be gone soon enough, leaving his family with a precious memory journey for Shelley. "Okay. But we don't have to pull photos out of the book. I'll get copies made at the drugstore."

Adam nodded. "Sure."

"I don't expect you to understand, but if you start pulling pictures out of that book it's like you're pulling out my heart. That book is special. It's a labor of love."

"I think getting a few copies made sounds great. We'll leave the book intact."

Just his tone indicated that he didn't understand. He never would. "And Adam, don't forget, Gavin's healing. I still haven't seen that smile from my boy. I miss it."

"At least you have something to miss."

She sucked in her breath.

"I'm sorry," Adam muttered. "I know I have to stop saying those things. I'm trying, Nicole. I really am. I just keep thinking of everything I've missed over the years."

And me missing you isn't even in your realm of thoughts, Adam Hawk.

Nicole kept her musings to herself as they went inside. In a few minutes, she had sent pictures from her phone to the drugstore. "The pictures will be ready tomorrow for pick up."

"Great."

They continued working silently for a few minutes, then Adam started texting on his phone. He looked up. "What are you doing for dinner?"

"Me?"

His gaze scanned the room. "There's no one else here. Of course you."

"Not sure. I have a few options in the fridge."

"Come to mom's with me. She just texted. Gavin is coming for dinner."

Why did all these normal daily activities slice through her like a just-sharpened knife? She couldn't help but think that the more time Gavin spent in the circle of Adam, the less time he would spend with her. Were these family gatherings necessary to his recovery? Would they put him any closer to climbing in an airplane? "Did she invite me? Or did you ask if you could drag me along."

"It doesn't matter who did the inviting. You're invited."

Maybe accepting the invitation this time would be helpful. It would give her a glimpse into the Hawk family dynamics and how Gavin fit.

How she didn't.

"Okay. What time?"

"We'll pack this up, grab Kylie, then you can ride back with Gavin."

"I need a minute to change," she told him.

"Go on. I'll box up our progress."

Nicole ran upstairs. She dug through the drawer, finding a stylish shirt. Brushing on mascara and blush didn't mean a thing. Just that she needed to look somewhat respectable. These days of cleaning out garages had her not looking into a mirror very often.

She straightened the barely-there wrinkles out of her shirt and slipped on festive flip-flops with tassels and bling.

Adam waited at the bottom of the stairs.

"Wow. You look pretty, Nicole."

She blushed and noted the tingle in her heart. "Thanks."

"But then again, you always look pretty."

Those words stopped her progress to the front door. "You don't have to say that."

"I know. I'm just speaking the truth."

She thought he was going to grab her hand, but instead he shoved his hands into his jean pockets, looking away momentarily before shifting his gaze back to her. "You've always been beautiful, Nicole, and to be honest I don't really know how I feel about you being back.

Trying to separate the 'me and Gavin' from the 'me and you' is difficult."

She swallowed hard. "It shouldn't be. There's no me and you, Adam."

The spark in his eyes sharpened. "In one sense, you're right. But in another sense...we had a child together. Seems like there should be some kind of bond."

"The bond has been one-sided for years." There. She'd said it. Her true feelings. He needed to know. Not that it would make a difference.

"Do I wish you would have told me about Gavin years ago? Yes. Can I predict how everything would have played out? No. But can I be of help in making decisions going forward? Yes. We have to start somewhere."

Her thoughts took her back to that month of May many moons ago. Her love for him had been real. Life changing. "It's not like we need to co-parent, Adam. Gavin is an adult."

"Adults still need advice and examples. You're asking me to help him find his love of flying again. What if that's not what he needs? What if it's love of life itself? I can talk planes and flying and all those things, but what if he needs more?"

"He needs you, Adam. I have to admit that."

"What if he needs both of us? What if all three of us need both of us?"

Nicole, Kylie and Shelley loaded the dishwasher and wiped down the counters after Gavin and Adam cleared the table, the dinner a little less awkward than Nicole had imagined. Tension between her and Adam hovered barely above water as the five of them ate a delicious meal made by Shelley.

Nicole stood at the kitchen counter and took stock of

the family room where Gavin and Adam had taken seats. Kylie played a game on someone's phone.

Shelley hung the dish towel on the oven handle. "Nice work."

She accepted every smile Shelley sent her way. While Nicole detected a hint of distance, the woman had seemed to come around from the last conversation they'd had. "It was a great meal. Thank you for inviting me."

As they walked to the family room, Adam's words replayed in her mind.

What if all three of us need both of us.

She hadn't answered him and hadn't pressed. What did the "both of us" look like?

The only thing standing in the way of an "us" was all those years of deceit. True, she'd never given him a chance to make a decision back then, but Adam becoming engaged to Rebecca so soon after prom made it clear where his feelings were.

With Rebecca.

Not with her.

The family room, full of coziness and comfort, also didn't include Nicole.

"I'm taking Kylie up in the plane tomorrow to Cincinnati to pick up parts. Anybody want to join us?" Adam spoke casually, like asking if anyone wanted a coffee.

"We're gonna have fun, Daddy. Gavin, do you want to come?"

The blank stare that had been Gavin's gaze since the accident stared back at Nicole, probably unrecognizable to the others. But Nicole knew.

What if all three of us need both of us? Adam's words hung in her mind. "I'll go." There. Solidarity. Now maybe Gavin would agree.

"Gavin? You up for it?" Adam's tone tried to be nonchalant but failed.

Shaking his head, Gavin looked down. "I have to do some online stuff with my résumé. Thanks anyway."

Nicole looked straight at her son. "We have to be out of the house. Mary is doing three showings tomorrow."

Gavin nodded. "Noted. I'll go to the coffee shop or the library."

"If you change your mind, I'm leaving at noon. I'll see you then, Nicole?" Did Adam's gaze look hopeful for her, or just hopeful that Gavin would change his mind?

"Sure."

Kylie looked up from her video game. "I wish you would come, Gav."

"Maybe next time, Punk."

Punk? Gav? Nicole balked at the familiarity these two had already. He'd never let her call him Gav. She'd tried a couple of times, but he asked her to call him Gavin. Witnessing these types of scenarios shattered Nicole's heart. "Gavin, we need to head out. There's some cleaning to do before the showings tomorrow."

Nicole wanted to make sure everything shined and sparkled for the prospective buyers. She needed to sell the Victorian and head back to Lincoln Park. Now more than ever.

Chapter Ten

"Kylie, watch your step as you get into the plane. Nicole, I'm right behind you." Adam motioned Nicole to follow Kylie's lead.

Nicole took a breath, wishing Gavin were here. Or Rachel. Anyone, actually. Was this a good idea? It seemed so homey, closely knit and everything else she wasn't when it came to the Hawk clan. She entered the plane, sitting in the copilot's seat and watched as Kylie buckled herself into the seat behind Adam's.

She hadn't realized how tight the space was in the plane. Why hadn't she volunteered to sit in the back?

"I wish Gavin was with us." Kylie's buckle clicked into place as she spoke, echoing Nicole's thoughts.

"Me, too, princess. Hopefully next time." Adam buckled up. "Are my girls ready?"

Nicole knew the term "his girls" was a general term, but it made her wonder. What if she was his girl? But she wasn't. She focused on the worst part of flying, the takeoff. In a matter of minutes, they were soaring. Nicole settled in as the plane reached its altitude.

"Isn't it amazing up here?" Adam, looking totally in his element, smiled at her.

A different kind of nervousness took over, but one that still made her stomach drop. Falling for Adam again would be dangerous. Nicole rested her hand on her knee, hoping the annoying knee bouncing would subside. "It's beautiful. I haven't been up in a small plane in years. For Gavin's tenth birthday, all he wanted was a plane ride. I saved every dime, and we went up with a local pilot. Oh, I forgot you already know all that."

Adam's gaze radiated regret as he looked at her. "I don't mind hearing you tell the stories."

"I don't know the story," Kylie interjected.

Nicole quickly relayed the birthday story to the six-year-old. "As much as I didn't want him to pursue flying, I did want to grant him his birthday wish. And since he'd never been in a plane before, a part of me thought 'What if he hates it?' That didn't happen. If anything, that flight made him fall in love with flying. He talked about it for weeks. That's how it became a tradition every year on his birthday until he went to college."

"If it's in you, it's in you." Adam pointed to the right. "See the river? That's Valley River that flows through Hawks Valley."

Nicole admired the way the river snaked through the terrain. Green foliage lined the edge, making a hedge-like boundary for miles.

Adam nudged her shoulder. "He'll fly again, Nicole. He just needs time. Look at how well he's doing with Kylie and Mom. And he's even been to the airport once. It's a start."

Nicole sucked in a breath as the combination of Adam's touch and words threatened to undo her. She took her phone out of her purse and snapped a couple of photos. "Not that he needs a reminder, but seeing a few pictures from this view couldn't hurt."

Still holding her phone, she turned the camera toward Adam. He glanced over, prompting her to snap a picture.

"Why are you taking my picture? So you'll have something to remember me by when you leave?" Adam's coy look indicated he was kidding around.

"Why are you leaving, Miss Nicole? Don't you want to stay with us?"

Her mind scrambled as Kylie's innocent words tore at her. "I have a home in Illinois. But I'm taking a picture because Gavin might like a picture of your dad." At least Kylie's question let her ignore Adam's insinuation, kidding or not.

"Okay. How about taking a selfie of all of us? It might encourage him." Adam leaned a little toward her, closing all space between them as their shoulders touched.

"It might, I guess." She tried to ignore their closeness and held her phone up. "Kylie, lean over." Nicole positioned the phone. "Ready?"

Nicole snapped the picture. Quickly, she made sure they were all in the photo.

"How does it look?" Adam asked.

Nicole held up the picture for him. "Fun. Like we're having fun. At least everyone is smiling."

Adam's gaze seemed thoughtful. "That's good. We *are* having fun, aren't we?"

"I am!" Kylie's voice piped in.

"Nicole?" Adam raised an eyebrow.

Nicole nodded. "Yes."

She placed the phone into her purse, ready to forget the image she'd snapped. Images. All of them. What was she doing up here in this plane with Adam and his daughter, subjecting herself to… What, exactly?

Torture? Visions of what would never be a part of her

life? She felt like an impostor..A fraud. A woman playing house—*playing* being the operative word.

The gentle roar of the engines and the scenery kept her occupied until they landed on a small airstrip. Adam helped her and Kylie out of the plane, then went back inside, this time exiting with a picnic basket. "My mom prepared this for today. Kylie, I think Grandma packed all of your favorites."

Nicole and Kylie guarded the picnic basket while Adam talked with the airport personnel. Gorgeous plane rides and family picnics shouldn't be in her schedule right now. She should be concentrating on the Victorian and the people wandering through it all day. There was a very real possibility of an offer when she returned. For so long it had simply been the thing that would happen eventually. In Lincoln Park, the sale seemed logical and practical. However, in Hawks Valley, the childhood memories blurred with her logical and practical decision.

Nicole replayed what she'd been telling herself since she'd been back. *I'll always have my memories, I don't need this house. Selling the house doesn't mean my memories will be sold.*

Adam's voice interrupted her thoughts. "Ready? They've got a car waiting for us. There's a cool park a couple of miles from here."

"Let's go."

He picked up the basket, a folded blanket on top. "I hope you ladies are hungry. This thing is heavy." He placed the basket in the trunk and less than five minutes later, he pulled into a parking lot.

"I'm *so* hungry." Kylie grabbed Adam's free hand as they made their way to a beautiful, lush green grassy area next to a small pond which boasted a fountain in the middle.

Nicole followed, her appetite still fickle. Food sounded great but hit like a dough ball in her stomach. She and Kylie helped Adam spread out the blanket and then, together, they unpacked fried chicken, potato salad, pickles and lemon pound cake, of course. "Want some lemonade?" he asked, setting out three plastic cups.

"Sure." Lemonade sounded refreshing.

"I want some, too." Kylie kneeled on the blanket, her small hand wrapped around one of the cups.

He poured the lemonade, then handed out paper plates, plastic forks and napkins. "Dig in."

After Kylie took a chicken leg, Nicole grabbed one of the wings and small portions of the other delicious looking items Shelley had packed. "I hate that Gavin is missing this."

"The food or the flight?" Adam took a bite of the chicken thigh he held.

"Both. I would have liked for him to be here," she said, wishing she could be anywhere else, with anyone else but the handsome pilot and his darling daughter. These intimate family outings would only lead to regret and heartache. And she'd had enough of both to last a lifetime.

"He's missing some good food." Adam nodded toward the spread on the blanket. "And a beautiful day. He'll fly again, Nicole. It's going to take time, but I'm confident it will happen. I'll keep pressing, in a good way of course."

True to form, the food rolled around in her stomach. She'd started this roller coaster of a situation, and everything seemed stalled on the peak. Gavin, while spending time with Adam and the rest of the family, hadn't made progress in the area of flying. The Victorian could sell at any moment, which left Nicole feeling at odds instead of thrilled. Nothing and everything was happening simultaneously which threatened to upend her world, as if sitting this close to Adam hadn't already started that process. He was twenty-five years more good-looking, wise and understanding. All the characteristics she'd fallen in love with as a teen. Then on a whim, in a swift change of a situation, he'd said good-bye.

No way could she risk her heart like that again.

Adam thanked God for the beautiful day and the chance to spend time with his daughter.

He also prayed he would be strong where Nicole was concerned. He had planned this plane ride and picnic not only to entice Gavin into being back in the air, but also to take steps toward building their family—a different family than the one sitting on the blanket. But when everyone agreed except Gavin, he just couldn't uninvite Nicole.

Could he?

Didn't matter now. He hadn't rescinded his invitation, and here he sat on a flowered blanket with his daughter and Nicole. The fact that this felt right pricked him, causing him to push any long term scenarios that included Nicole aside. Adam knew now more than ever that he couldn't rely on his feelings.

He'd been blind where Rebecca was concerned, and Nicole, too, for that matter. He couldn't fix anything with Rebecca, but he could keep his emotional distance from Nicole. He just had to concentrate on Gavin. Focus on spending more time with him, with Kylie and his mom.

He also needed to concentrate on seeing Gavin's love of flying return. A love Adam hadn't seen, but Nicole promised existed.

If only the sense of longing for more would leave him. Longing for a life that was out of reach, that stared him in the face in this park, that sat on a pretty blanket, in a grassy field. But like Nicole, pretty blankets and lush, grassy fields could be deceiving.

"Grandma cooks the best food, doesn't she, Daddy?" Kylie licked her fingers instead of using the napkin in front of her.

Adam nodded, glad for his daughter's interruption. "She does. Are you full?"

Kylie shoved the last bite of pound cake in her mouth before nodding.

"Nicole?" he asked. "Did you get enough to eat?"

She nodded. "More than enough. Thank you." She started to grab her drink, but her plate shifted and in the process of trying to steady it, she tipped her drink over onto Kylie's foot and sandal. "Oh, I'm sorry, Kylie." She grabbed her napkin and started rubbing the child's ankle.

"It's okay, Miss Nicole." Kylie grabbed her unused napkin and started helping Nicole. They both began laughing and Kylie started wiping Nicole's leg even though nothing had been spilled on it.

Nicole looked at his little girl. "Hand me your sandal. I'll wipe the sticky lemonade off of it."

"Okay." Kylie unstrapped her sandal, her huge smile never leaving her face, and handed her shoe over. "Here."

Nicole grabbed a bottle of water and poured some on a clean napkin. "This should do the trick."

Kylie giggled. "I like you, Miss Nicole. You are fun. And pretty. Isn't she pretty, Daddy?"

Adam started shoving items into the picnic basket, the camaraderie of Kylie and Nicole putting him on edge. This was a bad idea. He couldn't let Kylie become attached to Nicole in any way.

"Daddy? I asked if you thought Miss Nicole was pretty."

Adam looked at his daughter, her question cementing

all the reasons he and Nicole could never have a future. Situations like this would only give Kylie a false perception. "Yes, she's pretty. Like Grandma is pretty and Aunt Rachel is pretty." He tried to keep his tone light, but he saw Nicole stiffen as she finished wiping Kylie's sandal.

He needed to be more careful. Bringing Kylie into these scenarios would only lead to letdowns. And they'd already had their share of disappointments.

Nicole held out the sandal. "Here, Kylie. You can put this back on. Let's help your dad with this blanket."

"I've got it." The busier he was, the less his mind had time to roam. But nevertheless, it did roam to the selfie Nicole had snapped earlier in the plane. Smiles and coziness. A misleading photo.

Nicole and Kylie stood to the side as Adam pulled the blanket close to him before folding it in a manner his mom would question. "Let's go."

They walked the distance to the car in silence, a silence which continued on the short drive to the airport hangar. "I have to go in and grab the parts I came for. Kylie, come with me. You can throw this away." They exited the car, and he handed his daughter the small plastic bag that held their trash before turning to Nicole. "We'll be right back."

He grabbed his daughter's hand as she skipped alongside him, oblivious to the atmosphere that had shifted during the picnic. He wasn't sure which grew stronger. His resolve to help Gavin, or his resolve to keep Nicole at a safe distance from his family.

Adam hadn't been able to keep his mind off Nicole after their outing yesterday. Her all too easy rapport with Kylie and guarded eyes where he was concerned haunted him all night into today. The trip revealed all the reasons he should keep his distance. Besides, the Victorian would probably sell quickly, and Nicole would be back to her life.

Her life without him. He looked down at Kylie, who was standing next to him on Nicole's front porch. These actions defied his good judgment, but they were necessary, as he'd started the process of putting together the album for his mom, and he promised Kylie she could help. He wouldn't break his promise to his daughter, even though he had second thoughts about including Nicole in the process. The sooner they had the album finished, the sooner he could move on. He knocked on the door.

Nicole answered, her natural beauty taking his breath away. "Hi. Come on in."

Adam stepped in behind Kylie, reminding himself to keep this casual. This was a time for making a gift for his mom, not for wishing for things that could never be. "Thank you for letting us invade your home to finish the album. We appreciate it."

"Everything is set up in the kitchen," Nicole said, shutting the door behind them.

They made their way through the foyer, her scent lingering, taking his traitorous mind places it didn't need to go. All this familiarity—Nicole, her house, the time spent together—threatened to uproot his everyday world. And he knew firsthand where familiarity led. He'd let familiarity with Rebecca cloud his decision-making all those years ago. Just because something or someone was familiar, didn't mean it was right. At least he knew that now and could stay strong, regardless of where his mind wandered.

"Gavin!" Kylie ran to her half brother and hugged his legs while Gavin ruffled her hair. "Hi, Punk. What are you doing here?"

"We're making Grandma a present. Daddy said you were helping." She grabbed his hand and dragged him to the breakfast table where the album lay open.

Adam looked at Gavin. "Round two on the album." He dropped a plastic bag on the table. "This time, we brought colored pens that sparkle. Time to add some words to these memories."

"We're going to surprise her at her birthday party." Kylie gazed at her big brother. "You're coming, right?"

Adam wondered how anyone could refuse those big blue eyes.

Gavin shoved his hands in his jean pockets. "We'll see."

"Gavin, your mom has graciously said we could use some photos of you in the album. Would you like to help us choose which ones? She made some copies." Adam glanced at his son, hopeful he'd answer yes.

"I'm going to be in the book?" Gavin asked in surprise.

"Of course, brother. You *have* to be in the book." Kylie patted the chair next to where she sat. "Come sit and help me. Daddy said the book has to have a poe-sonal touch."

"I think he means *personal*." Gavin slid into the seat next to her.

Adam took a deep breath at the scene in front of him. The scene that still seemed surreal. His daughter and his son.

His son.

The words rolled through his mind easier but they were still swimming, somewhat. He slid into a chair next to Nicole. "Thank you again for all your help."

"I'm not doing much." She separated pictures scattered on the table. "Remember to leave room for writing. And Gavin's pictures are in the envelope."

"I want to write some memories for Grandma." Kylie

dug through the bag, pulling out the pens. "I like purple. And it's glittery."

Adam opened the pens and handed Kylie a purple one. "Here's a picture of you as a baby. What would you like to say to Grandma?"

Kylie tapped the pen to her chin, her gaze turned upward. She turned to Adam. "How about I loved her from when I was a baby."

They all laughed, and regardless of the circumstances, Adam knew these were times to cherish. "Sounds great."

Kylie started writing, but stopped, turning her gaze to Adam. "How do you spell 'loved'?"

He pointed to the paper. "Sound it—"

"What letter do you think it starts with?" Gavin interrupted. "Does it start with the letter P?"

Kylie giggled, wrinkling her sweet face, her attention fully on Gavin now. "No, silly. Not a P. An L."

Gavin smiled. "Yes. Now what's next?"

Adam, amazed at the patience Gavin had with Kylie, didn't notice when Nicole had left the table. When Kylie finished writing her sentence, and Nicole hadn't returned, Adam excused himself. "Keep up the good work, guys. I'll be right back."

Adam walked out of the kitchen and found Nicole in the sunroom. She stood by the window, her back to him. "Another penny for more thoughts."

"That expression is lame. No one says that anymore."

He took a step closer. "Yeah. Inflation. A dollar then?"

She turned, the early evening shadows coming through the windows. He thought back to high school. How did she still look like that same girl? Those feelings he started to feel all those years ago were more than scratching the surface now. He had to keep them at bay.

This whole situation with Gavin had everyone on emotional overload. On prom night, he'd let Nicole's kisses take him to unexpected places. He knew better now. Then why did the urge to kiss her, hold her in his arms and tell her everything would be all right, overwhelm him at this moment? But he no longer made promises he couldn't keep. And what he needed to keep was his distance. "Did you get any offers today?"

"No. But Mary said two of the three couples were very interested and she believes I'll see at least one offer in the next couple of days."

"That's good. It's a beautiful house."

"My mom made these curtains. They're still here."

"I can't imagine how hard this is for you. If there's anything I can do, let me know."

She sat on the sofa. "You can make sure my son goes back to flying planes. That's all I need you to do."

Nicole didn't move when he sat next to her. He took her hand. "You have to turn that over to God. I'll do all I can, but Gavin has to choose to fly again."

"God isn't in the habit of answering my prayers, so I'll leave that up to you as well." She released a long breath. "Entrusting my son's well-being to someone else isn't easy for me. It's been the two of us for so long."

Adam wondered if he would ever understand what it had taken for Nicole to tell him about Gavin after all these years. He saw God written all over this situation, but knew Nicole wasn't there yet. "I think you should give God another chance. It's true that He doesn't always answer the way we want, but He's a good listener and He cares about you."

"That may be your experience, but it's not mine." Her hand trembled in his.

He cupped her hand, saying a silent prayer for God to change Nicole's heart. To show her that He does love and care for her. "My gut tells me Gavin will come around in time. We just have to be patient."

"Time. It seems to fly and stand still. No pun intended."

As dusk settled, the shadows deepened and cast silhouettes on the wall. "Why don't you come back and help us finish this book? After all, you inspired it."

Nicole slipped her hand away from him. "You have the gist of it. Y'all are doing great."

Her tone, full of angst, worried Adam. "What's wrong, Nicole?"

She turned toward him, her big brown eyes swimming in sadness. "You all are a family now. I can see you growing closer every day. Gavin's even helping Kylie with her reading and writing."

While he wanted to understand her position, he found it difficult. "That's a blessing, don't you think? Considering how many ways the situation could have gone."

Nicole stood; then backed toward the doorway. "Don't you see? Gavin now has you and your family. So go. Be with your family. I don't begrudge you that. I promise."

Why did her words, that Adam couldn't have scripted any better if he tried, cause a pang in his heart? In that moment, Adam realized the scenario that he prayed for, the scenario that was being played out in real time in the next room, was the same scenario that would cause Nicole to hurt. She was stepping back, letting Adam be a family with his children.

Just what Adam wanted.

Then why did her actions unsettle him? Could there be a middle ground where he and Nicole were concerned? He hated seeing the hurt in her eyes and knowing he put it there. Adam closed the few steps between them, keeping his voice low like she had done. "You helping with the photo album means we're helping each other. That's all. It doesn't have to be complicated." He stayed just far enough away from her, yet her flowery scent still made him heady.

Wishful.

Confused.

Her arms wrapped loosely around her waist, her chin lifted slightly. "I don't want to lose my son."

With those words, she backed up a few steps, then left the room. He heard footsteps going upstairs, not toward the kitchen. She hadn't given him a chance to speak. A chance to say that no matter what the future held, he'd never take her son away from her.

And it saddened him to know that she thought he would.

Chapter Eleven

The offer loomed in front of Nicole. Over asking price. She just needed to sign her name. Then she could make plans to leave. She'd already inquired with a children's organization that would pick up the couple of beds that were here. The buyers requested the kitchen table and chairs be left for them along with the sunroom furniture.

Nicole tapped her fingers on the papers. This is what she'd been waiting for.

Now she could cut her ties with Hawks Valley. With Adam Hawk.

Kind of.

From this point forward, they'd be in touch regarding Gavin. But their son wasn't a child. In fact there may not be many reasons they'd have to be together. She remembered how she had to stand her ground a couple of nights ago. Everything she'd planned had started falling into place. But it felt different than she thought it would. Which was not in the plan. And then there was Adam himself.

She'd been burned by him before. Him acting like he liked her, then dumping her when Rebecca wanted him back. Her loving him and him thinking of her as a friend couldn't be repeated.

But now she was also the mother of his child. That came with its own special relationship. This house screamed of past relationships. Her mom and dad. Her friends. Years of having people over for dinner. Mom having the church ladies here every Wednesday night. Why did a few legal pages and a pen dredge up the past? Why did her mother have to die at such a young age?

She thought about what Adam said about God answering prayers differently than we wanted. Is that how He worked? It had been so long since Nicole had been to church. She glanced at her phone, noting the time. If she hurried, she wouldn't even be late.

Not understanding what truly propelled her, she quickly showered, touched on a bit of makeup, threw on a dress and ran a brush through her hair. She walked quietly past Gavin's room, not wanting to wake him.

Nicole slipped into her sandals before walking out the door.

The church bells rang at the top of the hour as she approached the steps. Right on time. She'd slide into the last pew and listen. What could it hurt?

As she entered the sanctuary, her mind raced to her childhood. The familiar stained glass windows down each side, the beautiful cross behind the choir loft, wrapped her in a comfort she hadn't expected. Burgundy pads still graced the wooden pews. Bibles, hymnals and offering envelopes within arm's reach. And the people. The organist started playing—a hint for everyone to find a seat. Nicole ventured no farther than the back pew. As she stepped to her left to sit, her gaze shifted to the front.

Her breath left her.

Adam stood holding Kylie's hand. He motioned Shelley into the pew, then his daughter went next. As Kylie sat next to Shelley, Adam slid in and right behind him, Gavin.

Gavin, looking like the spitting image of his father.

Nicole wanted to crumple then and there, but the big doors behind her had just shut with a loud squeak and she couldn't draw any attention to herself by opening them. She sat quickly, thankful the church had tissues on every row.

When had Gavin left this morning?

This situation spiraled before her eyes. She was losing her son. Now he attended church? Where the whole town obviously knew him. Why didn't anyone consult her?

A mom with a crying baby walked down the aisle. Nicole saw her chance and took it, slipping out behind the woman. But instead of following her down the green carpeted hallway, Nicole ran out into the sunshine, down the marble church steps, then headed to town. Rachel. Maybe she was working this morning? Nicole needed someone to talk to.

When she reached the coffee shop, she saw the Sunday hours: one to six. Nicole's fist tapped the glass. Of course. Rachel would give her employees a chance to attend church. Nicole stood in limbo—one foot in this charming town, the other in her simple life in Lincoln Park.

Catching her breath, she sat on a bench in front of the river, watching the people, the majestic river, all the aspects that made this town a popular tourist attraction. If it was so popular, why did Nicole want nothing to do with it?

She couldn't fly under the radar here.

How could Gavin be comfortable enough in such a short time to go to church with the Hawks? They had a pull on him. One she knew she couldn't fight. She'd brought Gavin here to be healed, not find a new family. She didn't see any healing being done regarding his flying, but she did see her son slipping into the Hawk dynamics day by day.

Nicole looked up. The bluer than blue sky, not a cloud gracing it, wouldn't hold her answers, she knew. But was God watching? God took her mother and father from her. Now He'd take her son. She could pray, she guessed. But for what? If God thought it best to keep Gavin in Hawks Valley, that's what would happen no matter how hard Nicole prayed he'd go back to his life with her.

I'm doing everything in the best interest for Gavin.

The words she kept telling Adam replayed in her mind. What if it was best for Gavin to stay in Hawks Valley? What if never flying again was best for him as well?

"How about a latte?"

Nicole shifted to see Rachel standing beside the bench, a coffee in each hand. "Rachel to the rescue." Nicole took the to-go cup, basking in gratefulness for the woman showing up just at the right time. She glanced at the sky once again, quickly. Was that God?

"I didn't know you needed rescuing, but I'm glad I could help." Rachel sat next to her, taking a sip of her coffee. "I saw you slip out of church, but I wanted to give you a few minutes. You saw Gavin with the Hawks, right?"

Nicole knew then that she could call Rachel a friend. Friends not only recognized wounded hearts, but they responded. "Yes. Gavin is a Hawk, isn't he? Somehow I keep forgetting the very thing I need to remember." Her whispered words resounded loudly in her mind. The truth somehow had a way of doing that.

Rachel grabbed Nicole's hand. "He's a St. John, too. You've done an amazing job raising him. You should be proud."

"I am. He seems to be bouncing back to life, but not in the way I imagined. He's finding his life in a new family, not in flying."

"Maybe the road to recovery is different than you thought, but it's still recovery." Rachel squeezed Nicole's hand.

"I'm scared." There. She'd admitted it.

"It's not a contest, Nicole. There's no winner and loser here, only people who love Gavin. How can being loved by so many people be bad?"

Nicole dabbed her eyes with what had become a well-used tissue. "My head knows you're right. But my heart fears… I don't know what exactly. Maybe that things won't ever be the same?"

"They won't. They can't. Again, that doesn't have to be a negative."

"The uncertainty of it all wrecks me. That's my baby boy."

Rachel smiled. "Your twenty-something baby boy. He'll never stop loving you, Nicole. You're his mom. You just might have to share him."

The woman's words were the root of the problem. *Share him.* With someone who chose another woman over her. Had she ever recovered from his choice? Would he ever recover from hers? "You're right, of course. I just need to sign the contract and leave town. All the nostalgia of returning to Hawks Valley, seeing Adam again, has me on edge and overreacting. Once I'm back home, I'll have a clearer head."

Rachel sipped her coffee before speaking. "I wish you would reconsider and stay. Hawks Valley is big enough for both you and Adam."

Nicole wrinkled her nose. "I don't know what to say. Moving here hasn't been an option for a long time. Besides, what are people going to think? Gavin attended church this morning with half of Hawks Valley. He looks just like Adam. I wish someone had asked me how I wanted to handle this."

"Handle what?"

"Gavin's introduction to the people here. They'll put two and two together quickly, then what will they think of me?"

Rachel waved her hand in the air. "Why do you care? You made the right decision at the time. End of story."

She sat straighter, slowly shaking her head. "Trust me. Everyone's stories will have their own made-up endings. Beginnings and middles, too. The nature of the small town."

"And the people coming alongside you are the blessings of the small town. Embrace those who support you and forget the rest."

Nicole knew Rachel's words were wise and worth thinking over. "I appreciate you skipping church to talk to me. I will miss your friendship when I'm back home."

Rachel sighed. "You keep saying back home. Back. Is that really the direction you want to move in?"

Nicole's coffee cup shook at Rachel's insight. "I don't know. I'm in unchartered territory."

Rachel draped her arm around Nicole. "You may be, but you're not alone. Just remember that."

She wished she could believe her friend. But sometimes, no matter how many people rallied around, the black hole of aloneness still loomed like an abyss waiting to be stepped into.

Adam surveyed his kitchen, the family just finishing lunch. If someone had told him a few days ago that this would be happening today, he wouldn't have believed them. But here they were.

His mom, his daughter.

His son.

Adam watched his mom pour Gavin another cup of coffee.

The afternoon lingered lazily. Shelley left after lunch, and Kylie, Gavin and Adam had hung out. Gavin had spoiled Kylie by playing one of her favorite video games while Adam took every detail of his family in. His cell rang. "Hi, Riles. Just a minute. Let me go somewhere quieter." He stepped outside, away from the friendly rivalry Kylie and Gavin were dishing out to each other. "What's up?"

"I wanted to give you a heads up. Did you know Nicole came to church this morning?" Riles asked.

Adam raised his eyebrows. "She did?"

"Yes. Didn't stay long, though. She sat in the back row—you know, like me—except on the other side of the church. But only a couple of minutes after she sat down, she left. Kind of ran out, by the looks of it."

He scratched his head at this information. "I wonder what happened to make her leave."

"I might have a clue. She left right after her gaze locked on you. And Gavin."

"Oh." Regret fell like dominoes through Adam. Of course. She probably saw them all together. Should he have invited her? No. Not after their last couple of outings. He needed to keep his family from becoming too attached to someone who had plans to leave.

Nicole would be heading back to Chicago just like she did all those years ago.

They had their moment. It passed. Could there be another moment? Another time? A second chance? That would be the surprise of all surprises. No matter how much that thought had his heart racing, he knew it wasn't possible.

"Just thought you should know." The older pilot's tone held concern.

"Thanks for the info. I appreciate it. You're a good man, Riles."

"So are you, Hawk. Maybe something's going on with her. Might be the Lord tugging at her heart. That's what He does."

Adam briefly looked up, like there would be a confirmation in the sky. "I hope so. I truly do. Again, I appreciate the info. See you tomorrow."

He walked back inside, not sure what to make of Riles's call. Was God moving in her heart, strengthening a desire to know Him? Would seeing them all at church really cause Nicole to run out?

"Daddy! Can Gavin take me to my dance lesson? Please? He said he would."

Dance lesson? Oh, yeah, the private lesson he'd arranged with Lark. He'd forgotten about it, actually. "Sure. Gavin can take you, and I'll pick you up. Go put on your dance clothes."

Kylie set her video controller down, then hugged Adam. "Thank you, Daddy. Be right back, Gav."

Kylie ran up the stairs, half tripping on her way. "Be careful." He shook his head, watching her leave. "That was Riles on the phone," he told his son. "Apparently your mom came to church this morning."

A confused expression crossed Gavin's face. "She did? She never goes to church."

"That's what I've heard." He shoved his phone in his pocket. "I appreciate you taking Kylie to dance class."

"It's not a problem. I told those guys I met at church

this morning I'd meet them for pizza anyway. So I'll take her on my way."

"Sounds good. Those are nice guys. Coached them in flag football years ago." He glanced at his watch. "And, since you are taking Kylie, I'm going to run over to your mom's. Talk with her."

"You mean find out why she went to church." Gavin smiled.

"Maybe."

After making sure Kylie's backpack had everything she needed, Adam said his good-byes to his son and daughter. *Son and daughter.*

He still couldn't fathom how much his life had changed. All because of Nicole. Right now he wanted, no needed, to find out why she ran out of church. Find out if God was tugging at her heart. But as he drove to her house, he couldn't come up with a subtle way to approach the subject. He exited his truck, then knocked on the door.

She opened it, glancing behind him. "Where's Gavin?"

"He went out for pizza."

"Okay. Come on in, I guess. Is something going on?"

"That's what I want to know. Did you run out of church this morning?" He sucked in a breath at his words. It was one thing to not be subtle, but he hadn't intended to be so blunt.

She stood looking like the girl from high school with her denim shorts and Hawks Valley High T-shirt. "Where'd you hear that?"

"Where'd you find that shirt?"

Nicole looked down, running her hands over the faded red shirt. "I found it in one of the boxes. It still fits. But stop trying to change the subject. Who told you about church?"

"I have friends. What gives?"

"You tell me. I thought Gavin was asleep, but no. I show up at church and there all of you are in practically the front row. How did you introduce him to people?"

He let a breath out now, understanding her sudden flight. "I introduced him as Gavin St. John. People are probably burning up phone lines, but that's their business. He wanted to come with us and we wanted him to come to church. He's already met some guys. In fact, that's who he's out with right now."

Nicole crossed her arms. "I'm so confused. We're not ever going to address the elephant in every single place we go in town?"

"I'm not making an announcement in the paper if that's what you mean. This will flow how it flows. One day at a time. There will be good days and not so good days. We'll handle them one at a time."

She leaned against the kitchen counter. "Easy for you to say. You're the wounded one. I'm the vixen who kept a secret for years." She held her hands up. "Hey, but what do I care? I'm leaving soon. There's an offer on the house. I just need to sign and I'm out."

"Nicole, we're both wounded. And I care what happens to you. How you feel." He walked to her, taking her hands in his. "Let's not project what people are going to say and do onto the situation." He considered it a small victory that she didn't pull away from him. He could feel her tenseness in the touch of her fingers. Adam wondered if she could feel his.

"Have you even talked to him about flying?" Her voice came out quiet. Soft. Like she knew the issue spanned more than Gavin flying.

Adam took a deep breath, dreading this conversation

as well. "When it comes up naturally, I do. Maybe that's not what he needs right now."

Those words caused her to strip her hands from him. "Oh. So you know him a few days and suddenly know what's best for him?"

Adam retreated a couple of steps. "I'm not saying that. He's becoming more comfortable around me, Mom and Kylie. He's making friends."

"He needs to make money. He needs a job. A flying job."

Adam rubbed his neck, her sense of urgency not escaping his notice. "Nicole. I'm trying to navigate this situation. You've dealt with the day-to-day routines, so I understand where you're coming from. But I haven't even really gotten to know him yet."

"I understand, but he can't stay unemployed forever." Nicole's stare challenged his. "I feel out of control."

Adam mentally tried to consider her concerns. He understood her desire for Gavin's future. Understood her need for normalcy. But nothing was normal. "We have to let things happen naturally. That may take time."

"Time I don't have. This buyer wants to move in at the end of the month. They have cash."

She shifted her weight, her bare feet taking him back to summers long ago. And now, one specific summer. Cold seeped through him at her words. A gentle yet strong reminder of where they stood. Where they would always stand. "That's fast."

She sighed, walked over to the table and plopped into the chair. "Everything is happening fast. The sale of the house. Gavin hanging out with your family. And now he's making friends here."

"All things that need to happen for everyone to move forward. I guess you're going to sign that offer."

"Yes. I'm taking it to Mary tomorrow."

The St. John Victorian would really belong to someone else. Unthinkable. "It's strange knowing you're selling the house. Even though you haven't been here, it's still always been your house. Now, it'll belong to someone else."

"Don't make me feel guilty. I don't need this house."

"Do you need the money?" he asked.

"No. It's going into a trust for Gavin."

Adam nodded. "Does he have to be a certain age to access the money?"

"No. I'm going to talk to him about it. I want him to use it wisely, like buying a house, a plane, something he'll enjoy and make memories with."

He better understood her reasoning for selling now, but it still messed with his heart and mind at how determined she really was to cut all ties with this town. With him. She'd have no reason to come back to Hawks Valley once the Victorian sold. "That's good, Nicole. A St. John legacy."

"I'll talk to him when he comes home. Tell him about the offer."

"Can I stay for that conversation? The future is bound to be brought up. Maybe we can see where his head is in regard to his next steps. You said he was unemployed. I thought he had a job."

Nicole shook her head. "He did. But when his boss wouldn't give him the week off to come and help me, he quit. That's why he showed up early."

These facts nudged Adam toward Nicole's line of concern. Idleness didn't lead to productivity. But he didn't want to jump to conclusions either. Gavin had secured a job after the accident. He'd only been unemployed a few days.

Nicole reached over, taking his hand in hers. "Yeah, I'd like it if you stayed to talk to him."

Oh, the promises her hand held. But only in his mind. He stared at the legal papers, the ones that would take Nicole out of Hawks Valley.

Out of his life.

Chapter Twelve

Nicole heard a car door slam. "Gavin's here."

She quickly removed her hand from Adam's, not understanding why her nerves suddenly took over. It was Gavin. Her son. Glancing at Adam, she smiled and sighed. A part of her was thrilled that he'd stay to talk to Gavin, but another part of her hoped her son wouldn't see this as them ganging up on him.

Gavin came in through the kitchen door, stopping short as soon as he stepped in. Nicole noticed his reluctance as he shut the door behind him. She walked over to him, giving him a hug. "Hi. Adam said you had pizza with some friends."

"Just some guys I met this morning. So were you at church?"

Nicole met his gaze head on. "Yes. For a little while."

"I thought church wasn't your thing." Shoving his keys in his pocket, he half smiled.

"I'm not opposed. I went to church until I graduated high school."

Gavin glanced back and forth between them. "For you two telling me you're not a couple, you sure do hang out a lot. Don't you have to pick up Kylie?"

"We had some things to discuss." Adam glanced at his watch. "I have a few minutes. Would you like to sit?"

Nicole couldn't decide if she liked Adam taking charge when it came to Gavin. It had been her role for so long.

Gavin slid onto the bench, his back to the bay window and the beauty outside. "What's going on?" he asked.

"I have an offer on the house." Nicole put her hand on the papers. "It's over asking and all cash. Can't ask for more than that."

Gavin didn't flinch. "Okay. That's why you came here, right? To sell the house?"

"Yes. But this means we'll be leaving soon. They want to close fast, and since it's a cash offer. It's possible."

Shrugging, Gavin swiped the screen on his phone. "Cool."

Nicole locked gazes with Adam.

"How does that look for you, Gavin?" Adam scooted back his chair and crossed his legs.

A puzzled look greeted Nicole and Adam as Gavin looked up from his phone. "I don't know. I'll figure it out then. Do you want me to go pick up Kylie?"

Adam's fingertips tapped the table as a curious look came over his face. "I've got it. But how about sticking around here for a few days? The Hawks Valley Fourth of July celebration is always amazing, and they give the Paul Hawk Award out at the ceremony before the concert. I always take the week of the fourth off and thought we might hang out."

Nicole sucked in a breath. What was this family-type banter about picking up Kylie like it was everyday life? And that suggestion for Gavin to stay? Why hadn't Adam shared these proposed plans with her? It's not like they hadn't sat here for a while and talked about Gavin's future. Never once did Adam mention their son staying after she left.

"What's the award for?" Gavin asked.

"They give it out every year to someone who has been instrumental in helping the community. My dad was on his way to bring in a special guest when his plane went down. It was the morning of the fourth."

Nicole noticed the hitch in Adam's voice. Even after all these years, it was hard to talk about. She understood.

"That sounds like a sad day. Yet you still celebrate the fourth?" Gavin pushed his phone to the side.

"It's bittersweet for sure. A day of remembrance. A day of celebration. I would like for you to be here, if you can. We would represent three generations of pilots."

Nicole kept her expression neutral as her insides crumbled. Adam wanted to share the important day with Gavin because he was important to him. The disappointment that ran through Nicole mirrored the very disappointment she'd vowed she'd never subject herself to again.

Yet here she sat, once again, not included in Adam's life.

Gavin looked at her. "What do you think, Ma? Would you mind if I stayed awhile? I wouldn't mind learning more about Grandpa Paul. He sounds like a great guy."

She didn't know what she minded anymore. But she couldn't think of a rational reason to make him come home. "If you want to stay, that's fine."

As she said those words, a dreaded scenario entered her mind. What if he didn't come back to Illinois? No. That couldn't happen. This conversation had taken a wrong turn and needed to be righted. "Except what are you going to do about a job, Gavin? Have you been looking at all?"

Gavin shimmied in his seat. "I've been weighing my options. Deciding what I want to do."

Nicole gave Adam's shin a gentle kick under the table. He took the hint. "What do you think you'd like to do? Weren't you flying cargo for a small transport company?"

Refusing to meet Nicole or Adam's gaze, Gavin glanced down at his phone once again. "I was. But I don't want that job back."

"Your mom is right. You need to line up something soon."

"I'm frugal. I have savings."

"Money is not the only benefit of having a job." Adam sat straighter. "I know guys who stayed out of work awhile, then found it hard to return. They became used to not working."

Gavin looked at him. "I'm not that guy. It's not that I don't want to work. Ma needed me here and they wouldn't let me off. It won't be hard to find something."

"Is 'something' what you want?" Adam folded his hands on the table. "Do you have a career path you're on?"

Gavin raised his eyebrows. "Dad 101? I'm not going to stay unemployed, if that's what you mean. I can and will support myself. Don't worry."

Nicole could see this conversation spiraling quickly. "Gavin, you owe Adam an apology. We're only asking these questions because we know what you're capable of."

"Do you want to fly again?" Adam looked at Gavin, not breaking his stare.

"A job is a job." Gavin's tone dared a rebuttal.

"A job isn't a job if you love what you do. Your Mom says you've lived your whole life to fly. Is that still true?"

Nicole watched the proverbial ball ping from one court to the other as Gavin and Adam battled words, not sure if Adam's direct approach would be effective.

"I don't want to talk about flying. I will land a job when I get home." Gavin slid to the end of the bench and got to his feet. "I can take care of myself. I don't need you watching over me like you do Kylie. In case you can't tell, I'm twenty-four. She's six. Big difference."

Nicole sat stunned at her son's defiance as he left the room. "I'm sorry, Adam. This behavior is what I'm talking about. This isn't like Gavin. He's always been respectful, thoughtful, loving."

Adam nodded. "I believe you. I've seen those attributes from him."

"And where do you come off asking him to stay? Why didn't you talk to me about that possibility first?"

"I didn't think it would be a problem. It's just a few days. Is it a problem?"

Nicole crossed her arms. If she told him her fears, what would he think? Would her fears plant thoughts in his mind that weren't already there? Would Adam guess her feelings were hurt? "I didn't know about the award. That's an honor for your family, I'm sure."

He nodded. "It is. My mom and I present it every year. I think it would be nice for Gavin to learn more about my dad. Our family flying history. But you didn't answer my question. Do you have a problem with Gavin staying on a few days?"

"I don't want to leave here without him." That situation made her insides curl.

"Why? He'll be here less than a week after you leave."

After you leave. Just like all those years ago, he wouldn't mind her leaving. It's ironic that she chose to come here at this time of the year. The time when the memories that tore her apart prevailed most. And here she sat, subjecting herself to the same scenario.

What bothered her more? Adam not caring if she left

or Gavin staying on without her, being a part of the family she'd dreamed of belonging to?

When did all her fears run together?

This is what being around Adam Hawk did to her. Confused the lines.

The narrative.

Which is why the offer needed to be signed and she needed to be gone. Her heart couldn't take another rejection from Adam.

Adam watched Nicole. Gavin's reaction seemed typical of a young man hurting. She didn't need to apologize for him. But somehow she felt responsible. Like his actions were a reflection of how she had raised him. Adam knew better.

Since she didn't answer the question he'd asked twice, his gut told him not to ask again. Either she had no logical answer, or she didn't want to tell him the real reason she didn't want to leave without Gavin. "Look. Nothing has to be decided today. Let's see how this plays out. I know you're leaving at the end of the month. If there's anything I can do to help you with getting this house in order, let me know, I'd be happy to help."

She glared at him like he'd just offered to wreck every single one of her plans, not help facilitate them.

"I'll be fine. But thank you."

Adam's phone dinged. His insides cringed as he read the text. "I've got to go. Lark just texted that Kylie's just injured her foot." He scrambled from the table, shoving his phone in his pocket.

A look of concern etched Nicole's expression. "I hope she's okay. I'd be happy to come along."

"You hope who's okay?" Gavin asked, standing in the doorway.

"Kylie." Adam pushed his chair up to the table. "She hurt her foot at dance. Lark said she probably needs to go to the ER."

Gavin's eyes widened. "I'll go with you, you know, in case you need somebody to drive or hold her, or something."

Adam's heart swelled at Gavin's generosity toward Kylie. "Great. I'd like that. Nicole, I'll text you when we know something."

Gavin followed him to the truck. He barely obeyed the speed limit while driving to Woodvale. When he and Gavin walked into the studio, Kylie sat against the wall with a tear-streaked face and an ice pack on her ankle. "Hi, princess. How are you doing?"

"It hurts, Daddy. Hi, Gav. I made a boo-boo."

"I see that, Punk."

Adam took off the ice and found an already bruised-looking ankle. "Doesn't look great. I guess we need to have a doctor look at it."

"I don't want to go to the doctor, Daddy. They'll give me a shot."

Adam chuckled. "Not necessarily. But we need to see how badly it's hurt."

Lark walked over carrying Kylie's backpack. "Hi. I'm so sorry about this. We were doing a jump move and she just landed wrong. I hope it's not broken. I put her shoes in here." She handed Adam Kylie's purple backpack before her gaze landed on Gavin. "I don't think we've met. I'm Lark Woodvale."

"Hi. I'm Gavin St. John. Nice to meet you."

"You, too. Weren't you staying here a few days ago?"

Gavin nodded. "I'm checked out now. Staying with my mom."

Adam couldn't hide a smile at the look on Lark's face. Oh, there'd be some talk at Woodvale when they left.

"That's cool." Lark nodded toward Kylie. "I won't keep you. Go get this girl checked out."

"Thanks, Lark. I'll text you with the outcome." He hooked the backpack on his shoulder. "Ready kiddo?"

"I'll carry her." Gavin scooped Kylie in his arms.

"Let's go." Adam knew no matter how Gavin felt about him or Nicole regarding the whole parenting thing, Gavin loved his little sister. He naturally gravitated toward her and instinctively wanted to take care of her. That's what families did.

Gavin's actions indicated he felt that strong family tie with Kylie. Adam wished he knew how Gavin felt about him, but those feelings might be harder to come by. He knew he had to be patient. Love, joy, peace, patience… Fruits of the spirit. He'd say prayers for sure regarding the patience aspect. Maybe Gavin would agree to stay the week of the fourth. And no, he wasn't trying to keep him here so he'd never go back to Nicole.

Simply, Adam wanted Gavin to experience the traditionally special time of year for the Hawks. Learn more about his heritage.

Five hours later, they left the ER, tired and armed with orders to see a pediatric orthopedic tomorrow. Kylie's ankle was indeed broken, and she'd need a cast. A quick trip in and out of the pharmacy for children's pain reliever made Adam appreciate Gavin being with them all the more. He also kept Kylie's focus off her ankle.

Adam saw the goodness of God in the compassion of Gavin, who helped settle her into bed and offered to read her a bedtime story. Hearing Kylie's giggles gave Adam's hurting heart a jolt of happiness.

He sent texts to his mom, Lark, Rachel and Nicole regarding Kylie's condition. He thanked them all for prayers and promised to let them know how her doctor visit went tomorrow.

His phone rang and he saw his mom's name. Swiping, he answered and put her on speaker. "Hi, Mom. I guess you got my text."

"I did. I'm so sorry this happened. Do you need me to cancel my trip?"

"Trip?" Adam smacked his head with his hand. His mom's annual birthday girl's trip. How could he have forgotten? "Uh, no. You go. Have fun."

"Weren't you putting Kylie in that weeklong camp? Can she still attend with her leg in a cast?"

"I'll work it out, Mom. I'm sure Rachel can help some. Don't worry. Just go and have a good time."

"I'll watch her."

Gavin had come downstairs and apparently overheard the conversation. "What?"

Gavin plopped onto the couch. "Maybe I can stay here for the week? I'll watch Kylie while you're at work."

A sense of family fell on Adam like never before. His daughter upstairs asleep, his mom on the phone and his son offering to help out in a bind. He thanked God. "See there, Mom? It's all worked out. Go enjoy the beach."

"All right, honey. Saying prayers for our sweet girl. Thank you, Gavin, for keeping an eye on her. She'll give you a run for your money, though."

Gavin smiled. "We'll see about that."

"Text me when your toes are in the sand, Mom."

She laughed. "I will. Love you. Both of you."

Adam set his phone down. "Thank you. I know Kylie will be thrilled to have you here." Not only Kylie. Adam found it hard to put into words, even in his mind, what it meant to him. But he'd keep his thoughts to himself. He would follow Gavin's lead and take this slowly.

"Not sure Ma will be, though."

"Your Mom will understand." Adam knew Gavin had to take Nicole's feelings into account. Maybe she would see it differently now that the situation was somewhat forced—with Kylie's injury and a need for Gavin to be here. A need was different than a want.

He knew that all too well.

Gavin set his phone on the coffee table. "I guess I'll grab my things and car tomorrow since it's so late."

"I sent Nicole a text a while ago. She hasn't responded."

"I texted her, too. She's probably asleep." Gavin flipped through the aviation magazine he grabbed off the table.

From what Adam knew about Nicole she wouldn't go to sleep without waiting for an update on Kylie. He didn't think she was asleep. No, she was more likely sitting and thinking up ways that Adam was trying to take Gavin away from her.

Nothing could be further from the truth. He would never take Gavin away from her. Adrenaline shot through his body.

How could he make her see? What did he need to do to convince her he didn't want to take *anything* from her, especially her son? Adam just wanted to get to know his son more and that couldn't happen without spending time with him. His mom and Kylie needed that time as well.

Kylie was already so attached, and Adam's heart threatened to burst whenever he saw them together. The brother Kylie never had. But Adam could also see an attachment forming with his little girl and Nicole that had the potential to hurt Kylie. Gavin going back and forth between Hawks Valley and Lincoln Park would be hard enough for his daughter, but Nicole's leaving would be permanent.

Like it was when she left all those years ago. The fact that she came back negated the word permanent, but this short time she was spending here was just a brief interruption in her long-term life in Illinois. Her job, her home and her friends—he assumed—would all be there to welcome her back when she returned.

Nicole had made it plain that Hawks Valley didn't feel like home. He now knew the why behind her silence all those years. Which gave Adam all the more reason not to trust her with anything regarding his heart.

Chapter Thirteen

Nicole thought she'd feel relief at having the offer signed, like a weight had been lifted off her. Instead, her mind whirled as she realized she only had a few more days to stay in this house before she had to leave.

And now Gavin would be staying with Adam to help with Kylie, a move she knew would come after Adam's text last night.

Nicole shoved another box to the side of the garage. She would be making a trip to the local thrift store to drop off the useable items. She had been surprised by the good condition of many of her dad's tools.

The people from the dump were coming this weekend to take everything from the garage and then the children's shelter would come to take the two beds that she offered to donate to them.

Other than the kitchen table and sunroom furniture, which the new owners had requested be left, the house would be empty.

Years of St. John history would meld into a new family's beginnings.

Nicole turned at the sound of a car pulling down the driveway. She recognized her realtor's car. However, she didn't know the two people who exited the car with Mary. She made her way to the group as she brushed dust off her shorts.

"Nicole." Mary gave her a hug as she greeted her. "I hope we're not intruding. This is Kent and Joanna Billings. They are buying your home."

Nicole smiled and shook hands with the couple who appeared to be of retirement age. "Nice to meet you."

"Likewise. You have a beautiful home. It captured our hearts and dreams the minute we drove into the driveway with Mary." Joanna's gaze lingered on the house after she spoke.

Although Nicole could tell they would love and care for the Victorian, it struck her that this was real. Her family home would soon belong to another family. Had she made the right decision? Putting faces to the new occupants didn't ease her sudden doubt.

"We hope you don't mind, but they wanted to walk through it again." Mary grabbed her purse from the car.

"No. Not at all." Nicole imagined them measuring rooms, picking colors, placing furniture. Maybe deciding what decor to use. She took a deep breath.

Joanna turned her attention to Nicole. "Would you mind joining us? If we're not interrupting you, that is. We'd love to share our plans for the house with you."

Nicole looked down at her grimy clothes. *Could she do this?* "If you don't mind my dusty self walking through. I've been in the garage all morning."

"Not at all." Joanna nodded toward the house. "Let's go inside."

Nicole grasped on to the older woman's take-charge attitude and followed Mary and the new buyers into the house.

"Now this living room is *fabulous*." Joanna walked

into the middle of the empty space. "I can see a seating area here," she said, standing before the fireplace,
"and also here." She walked over to the area beside the
big windows.

Nicole wondered why she'd want more than one seating area, but who was she to question this woman who
seemed to have a definite plan.

"Then I can see a huge round table over here." Joanna turned to her husband. "Round will be great, don't
you think? That beautiful oak table we saw that seated
twelve? I knew that table was meant for us."

Nicole's mind swam with visions of future family
gatherings, probably Kent and Joanna's grandchildren
running around. A big family hosting holiday gatherings, birthday celebrations. Even though Nicole knew
nothing about Kent and Joanna, their grand plans for the
home indicated either a big family, or a lot of friends.
Probably both.

Joanna's excitement tried to spill into Nicole's heart.
Tried to validate that she had made the right decision. Her
family home would no doubt be filled with joy and love
of people. But she had joy in this house. Joy that Gavin
never had the chance to experience.

As they migrated into the kitchen area, the conversation between Joanna and Kent continued, with plans to
update the countertops and add an industrial-sized re-
frigerator-freezer and a new sink.

"A farm sink for sure. And at this table," Joanna continued, resting her hand on the oak table by the bay
window, "we'll host guests for a special breakfast on cel-
ebratory days. We'll come up with a particularly quaint
menu for those occasions."

Nicole shifted her weight, hearing Joanna's words,
but not making sense of them. "What guests? Do you

host families for some reason? Charity work? Business associates?"

"No. We're turning this house into a bed-and-breakfast. I mean we hope to. We're looking into the process now. We know Woodvale is popular, but there are times when even they are booked. We just want to offer a quaint, close to downtown, Hawks Valley experience."

Chills ran down Nicole's arms at the woman's words. They were turning her home into a bed-and-breakfast?

Joanna ran her hand across the table in the breakfast nook. "We'd love to talk with you and learn some of the family history. We want to showcase this home with all of its beauty. And with the big corner lot, there's plenty of room for an outdoor area and parking."

"Wow. I don't know what to say. I never thought of my house becoming a bed-and-breakfast." Nicole wasn't sure how she felt about a constant stream of strangers walking the floors, eating in the dining room. Strangers having the opportunity to make the memories she had deprived her son of making. What had she done?

"It's a fabulous home and should be enjoyed by many." Joanna continued her wish list out loud.

Nicole's demeanor calmed as she noticed how Joanna and her husband didn't want to make any major changes. Keeping the home as close to original seemed to be a priority for them. The second floor took on a new meaning as Nicole walked through the four bedrooms, each with their own bathroom, and wondered what sort of codes had to be met to change this to a bed-and-breakfast.

Maybe too many.

But then she pushed those thoughts away, remembering she wouldn't be involved in this. They were buying the house from her, and she would be out of the picture.

She sighed. Everything in Hawks Valley had become

a life changing situation for her. Did her life need changing that much? Couldn't Gavin be a part of the Hawk family without moving in with them? Couldn't her house be sold to someone who wanted to live in it, not share it with the world?

Maybe her view of life, and its possibilities, was too small? Could she be the problem? Could her views and visions be less than what the world had to offer?

What God had to offer?

Why these thoughts about God? Where did they come from? She'd spent less than five minutes in a church over the last twenty years. But simply being around the Hawks, Rachel and those who lived their lives for God, made her feel closer to Him. They talked about their faith and their lives reflected their words.

She knew coming to Hawks Valley would be difficult. But never in her dreams could she have imagined all these life changing scenarios.

As they all walked down the stairs, Joanna still planning out loud, Nicole headed toward the front door needing fresh air. "I'm going to go finish in the garage."

"Thank you." The woman held out her hand. "I hope to talk to you more regarding

house. It's simply beautiful and I'm sure there are stories that need to be told. That personal touch would add so much to make each guest feel special."

Nicole quickly shook Joanna's hand. "Maybe we could talk sometime. And it was nice meeting you."

The hot summer afternoon air sucked the breath out of Nicole as she stepped onto the porch, but she needed to be alone. Out of the presence of the queen of planning, apparently. Her beautiful, simple house, turned hotel. Special, poignant memories to be made by strangers.

She slowly made her way to the garage—the task in

front of her coming to an end. Like everything else familiar in her life. Could she cope with so many changes? Could she leave Gavin here in Hawks Valley? Even for a week?

She drew in a breath as she felt the wet trails lacing her cheeks, honestly surprised at her tears. The level of detachment she thought she had regarding the sale fell away as she turned, letting her gaze linger on her childhood home.

Was she detached from anything regarding Hawks Valley? Or had this town and its occupants, one with dark hair and blue eyes in particular, wrapped her in a reality she thought impossible.

God was a God of possibilities.

Nicole pressed her fingers to the corners of her eyes wishing she believed that.

Adam shoved his hands in his pockets as he left the church office. Pipes bursting in the lower level of the church was never good, but now he had no place to host his mom's party.

Everything had been arranged for the celebration to take place in the fellowship hall, but the damage required new floors and that would take a couple of weeks.

The party was Sunday evening.

Not only did he need to find a new location, he needed to contact everyone.

He would start with Rachel. She'd been a big help planning the party. He made his way over to the coffee shop, relishing the feel of the air conditioning as he stepped inside. He spotted her sitting at a table.

With Nicole.

His heart jumped.

She'd always been beautiful, but he needed to remember that beauty didn't make a relationship. And he and Nicole didn't have what it took to navigate a romance.

But hey, maybe he could enlist her help with the party. They made it through putting together the picture album. Rachel and Nicole, his friends, could turn this bad situation into a fun party. He prayed that was the case.

"Hello, ladies."

They'd been so engrossed in conversation that they didn't see him walk up. He grabbed the back of a chair at their table. "Can I sit?"

"Sure." Rachel smiled and motioned for him to sit.

"How's Kylie?" Nicole asked, her voice soft, her gaze not meeting his at all.

"Yes, how's our girl doing with her cast and all?" Rachel chimed in.

"She's doing great. Gavin has been awesome. He's playing games with her, helping her maneuver around. He's a good boy, Nicole." Adam meant every word. Nicole had done a great job raising him, and Adam would be forever grateful to her.

"He is." Nicole picked up her coffee mug, steam still rising, yet he got the sense that there was more she wanted to say.

"Can I grab you a coffee, Adam?" Rachel nodded toward the menu.

"No. I actually have some unfortunate news to share."

Rachel tilted her head. "What happened?"

"Well, I just came from the church and they had a pipe burst downstairs."

Rachel covered her mouth with her hand. "Oh, no! Shelley's party. Can you still have the event there?"

Adam shook his head. "Nope. That's why they called me over. They wanted me to see the damage firsthand. No way it's going to be fixed by Sunday. They're sending out an e-mail. No Sunday school for a couple of weeks. So I need to not only find a place for the party—I need to contact everyone with the new location."

"When you find a new location." Rachel grabbed her cup with both hands.

"Exactly."

They all three sat in silence, not a good sign in Adam's opinion. "I've been trying to think of a place, but this is such short notice."

"What about Woodvale?" Nicole asked.

"If they had a room, which they wouldn't at this late date, it's too pricy. That's why I didn't contact them in the first place."

"Oh."

Nicole looked deep in thought. Adam didn't know why. She hadn't been around here for so many years, he wasn't sure she would remember places. Especially ones to host a party.

"I wish I had a bigger house," Rachel chimed in. "But the bungalow, while perfect for me, is so small. We'd be miserable in there. And the yard is still a hot mess. Mostly dirt."

Adam nodded. "At least we're throwing ideas out. Maybe the next one will stick."

Nicole sat straighter in her chair, pushing her hair behind her ears. "What about the Victorian?"

"The Victorian?" Adam and Rachel spoke at the same time.

"Is that a possibility?" Rachel asked.

"I don't see why not." Nicole sipped her coffee. "Can we borrow the tables and chairs from the church?"

Adam pulled out his phone. "I'll see. I'm sure they store them downstairs, but I'll send Sheryl a text. See if they are usable."

"I mean, the main floor is empty save for the sunroom furniture and kitchen table. We can set up the tables and chairs and food in the living and dining rooms." Nicole set her mug down, her smile and thoughtfulness pinging Adam's heart in ways it shouldn't.

Why did Adam's wayward emotions keep trying to betray his sound mind? His heart wanted to make something out of Nicole's kind gesture. And his mind knew that is all it was. Her generosity, even though he knew she wasn't happy with him regarding his invitation to Gavin, had outweighed her personal feelings. And for that, Adam was grateful. "I appreciate this so much, Nicole. It might work."

Her finger traced the design on the coffee mug. "Might as well have one last hurrah before I sell the place." She tilted her head. "Oh, and I met the new owners today."

"Yes, you did." Rachel smiled. "Tell Adam what they're doing with the house. That's what we've been chatting about."

Visions of bulldozers and new construction alarmed him. "What are they doing?"

"They're turning it into a bed-and-breakfast."

Those words were unexpected. "Really? They can do that?"

Nicole shrugged. "It will take time, but that's their plan. Joanna, that's the lady's name, has grand plans. She asked a lot of questions. I don't guess they can submit paperwork and get zoning until they own the place, but Rachel and I don't think they'll run into too many obstacles."

"Because they want to preserve the history of Hawks Valley." Rachel nodded toward the counter, then stood. "There's a line forming. I better go help. Let me know when we firm up plans. I'll help contact people. Thank you, Nicole, for offering up the Victorian. I think that will be amazing."

Rachel just said everything that had been brewing in Adam's mind. "She's right. Thank you for offering."

Nicole shrugged. "It's sitting empty. Everything is cleaned out. What time is the party?"

"At six."

"Okay. That will work."

Adam's phone dinged. "Sheryl says we can use the tables and chairs. Some of them were affected, but most weren't." He texted a thank you, then set his phone down.

"Sounds good. I'm glad everything is coming together."

Coming together for sure, Adam thought as his phone dinged again. "Uh-oh. Two steps forward, one back. Sheryl said all the decorations for Mom's party have been ruined. The boxes are waterlogged. Not good news." He knew nothing about decorating, but feared he might have to learn soon.

Nicole pushed her hair behind her ears. "What was the theme? Can you replace the decorations?"

He shook his head. "We'll have to talk to Rachel. She was in charge of decorating. Again, your offer of the Victorian is more than generous." He wished Nicole could be as generous in her thoughts toward him instead of thinking he was out to ruin her life at every turn. Her opinion of him obviously wasn't high, and he needed to remember that every time his heart threatened to overtake his mind.

"We'll set up the tables here." Nicole walked into the empty living room. "And back here—" she headed toward the dining room "—we'll set up the food table."

Nicole recalled Joanna parading around the house just

hours ago. Now here she was, parading around the same way. But for a different reason.

Shelley's party.

Adam's mother.

Gavin's grandmother.

Why had she offered her house? The pull toward the Hawks had always been great, but here she stood, with Adam, mapping out a game plan for his mother's seventieth birthday.

Nicole pushed her hair behind her ears. Maybe this could be an amazing memory for her and Gavin to hold close. To remember forever.

Adam stood next to one of the windows, his gaze surveying the room. When his soulful eyes connected with her own, her mind drifted to that long ago spring when, for a short time, he had been hers. A very short time, but long enough to make memories for a lifetime.

Memories she enjoyed but Adam only recently started making.

"I appreciate you offering your home, Nicole. It's really saving the day."

His words touched her. They sounded sincere. Dusk fell behind him, the darkening sky visible through the huge window.

"I'm just helping out however I can."

She held her breath as he walked toward her. "You're more than helping. You're generosity will ensure the special day planned for my mom is still memorable."

Nicole wanted to back up, but her feet refused to move, as if they were rooted to the floor. "Everyone's pitching in, doing what they can."

He stopped within arm's reach. "Yes. But no one would be doing anything if you hadn't come through with the Victorian."

Every emotion she thought she had buried regarding Adam resurfaced with a vengeance. She willed him not to come closer. Willed his strong arms not to embrace her, his gentle lips not to kiss her. She'd been here before with Adam. Years couldn't erase him from her mind, her soul.

What dangerous thoughts!

Now she willed her own mind to think realistic thoughts. But how could she, with the man who'd plagued her thoughts for so many years? Who was now standing close enough to touch?

To hold.

To honor and cherish.

What dangerous words! "Adam."

"Nicole." One step and a mirage of past mistakes separated them. She shut her eyes, seeing the short distance between them as the ocean it was.

Kissing Adam would risk her heart again. With regret, she turned away from him, as if the physical action would remove her emotional attachment. Dusk had fallen, sending shadowy vibes into the house, into her heart.

"Nicole. Don't walk away."

Walk away? "Oh, I won't. That's your job." The words sounded as bad out of her mouth as they had in her head, but she had to put up all defenses at this crucial time. Her heart and life hung in the balance. She refused to be hurt by Adam again.

"Touché. You're right. I did walk. But so did you. We can't escape the past, can we?"

"No, we can't. And it's true—I did leave—but I came back. You? You were unavailable. Now I have a life that I'm happy with and it's not here in Hawks Valley." Part of her heart tumbled as she spoke, but truth was truth. No matter who it hurt.

She could feel Adam's presence. "Things used to be so easy with us when we were friends."

Easy on him, maybe. She remembered the turmoil of keeping her true feelings at bay as he romanced Rebecca.

He stood so close that his breath caressed her neck. She wished he'd chosen her all those years ago. Maybe they would be living in the Victorian, planning this party for his mother together as a couple. As a happily married couple.

But no. He didn't choose her then and she had to make her own choices now. And being friends with Adam Hawk was proving more difficult than she thought.

Chapter Fourteen

Sun streamed in through the windows on what promised to be a beautiful day for Shelley's surprise party. Nicole watched as people placed the white chairs around the tables draped with poinsettia tablecloths in her home. The red, silver and white balloon arch fit perfectly in the living room. Red and white roses with festive greenery were placed in exquisite crystal vases, ready to be placed in the middle of each table.

The party, a labor of love from Shelley's friends and family, warmed Nicole's heart. She watched as Adam directed people with tasks to complete the setup. Her breath skipped as she thought of what he wanted to do today.

Introduce Gavin to the people at the festivities as his son. The big reveal.

Nerves filled her at the prospect, but she had no choice. The people helping with the party had been nice. Nicole didn't doubt anyone would be anything but welcoming to Adam Hawk's son. But how much further would this cement Gavin into the lives of not only the Hawks, but the town?

She would only be here a couple more days as the closing had been scheduled for tomorrow. Rachel had offered for Nicole to stay at her place since she wasn't leaving until the day after the Fourth of July celebration.

"Hi, Nicole. I'm sorry I'm late." Rachel gave her a quick hug. "Holly had a flat tire and I had to cover her shift until she arrived." Turning in a circle, she clapped her hands. "The place looks amazing. This is truly Christmas in July. Shelley is going to be so surprised. I parked way down the street like everyone else. Who is bringing her?"

"Gavin. Not sure what excuse he's using, but he's bringing Shelley and Kylie, who's moving around quite well in her cast." Nicole glanced at her phone. "We only have about one hour. Time is ticking down. The food should be arriving any minute."

"I set the coffee and everything to go with it in the kitchen. Christmas themed. Peppermint syrup and all."

"Thank you so much. Who doesn't love a good peppermint latte in July?"

Rachel ran her hands down her red summer dress. "I know, right?"

"And that tree, girl." Nicole pointed to the tree Rachel used at her coffee shop and had graciously loaned them for the party. "Your coffee shop must look amazing at Christmas time."

"It wouldn't be Christmas in July without a tree. Thank you for offering the Victorian when the church fell through. How fitting to throw a final hurrah here before you sell."

Her friend spoke the words Nicole had been thinking for days. This was such a great house. But it was beyond time for her to move on. And how special that her final memory of the house would be with Gavin, and a host of people, celebrating a great woman. She could now let the house go without regret. If only thoughts of Adam would quit invading her mind.

Stop! She had to rein in those Adam thoughts. This birthday party, while whimsical and fun, couldn't be further from real life. Just as Christmas did not happen in July, she and Adam could never be a couple.

"Looks like Christmas exploded in here. Mom is going to be stoked."

Nicole closed her eyes momentarily at the sound of Adam's voice. That happened a lot lately, causing a tug-of-war in her heart. But again, she couldn't allow herself to be carried away by kindness. The kindness she had hoped for when she told Adam about Gavin. "I hope so. Everyone has pitched in wonderfully. And it's such a beautiful day outside. Like the weather knew we were throwing a party. We set up chairs in the backyard as well as a couple of tables. Last minute addition. Along with another surprise."

"Oh? What's that?"

Nicole thought of her twinkling light surprise. "You'll have to wait and see."

He nodded toward the living room. "What do you think of those stockings? Brought them from home. Hung them myself. And I have my own surprise for later."

Nicole took in the two stockings hanging from the mantel. "Nice. They're not centered, but if that's how you roll, it looks perfect."

Adam smiled, his fingers lightly squeezing hers but only for a moment. "It's how I'm rolling today. At least for a little while." He took her hand in his, twirling her around once, like they were dancing. "Green is your color."

"Thank you." Being with him like this took her breath away, but Nicole couldn't allow herself to become swept up in the moment. She needed to stay grounded in her mission. Gavin. Her heart still lurched at the thought of him staying on without her, but she held on to the belief that he would come back to the town house soon. Although he was old enough to live on his own anywhere in the world, living in Hawks Valley would take a part of him from her that no other city in the world would.

"Nicole, the caterer is here." Rachel walked up, pointing to the kitchen.

"Great. Do you want to help me set up?" She motioned for Rachel to follow, leaving Adam standing in the foyer.

Rachel shook her head. "I'm working on hanging the happy birthday banner. Maybe Adam will help you."

He moved in that direction. "Sure. Let's go."

Nicole followed, trying not to focus on how GQ Adam looked in his gray slacks and white polo, which he wore loose and untucked. A perfect style choice for summer.

Who was she kidding? Everything he wore turned into a perfect style choice.

Within twenty minutes, with the caterers help, they had the buffet, coffee bar and dessert table in place. Christmas plates and napkins helped set the tone.

"Did you crank the air down to sixty?" Adam asked, rubbing his arms.

"Yes, I turned it down, but believe me—we'll need it when everyone arrives. Which should be in about fifteen minutes. Your mom should be here in half an hour."

"Almost showtime. The place looks amazing, Nicole. Thank you." He reached for her hand, pulling her close to him.

Nicole didn't step away, the festive atmosphere making her vulnerable. "It's quite magical having Christmas in July."

"You've made it all possible." His words whispered in

her ear sent tingles down her spine and a longing into her heart. A longing that continued the tug-of-war inside her.

"Shelley is Gavin's grandmother. This day needs to be special." Her hand still held on to his as she breathed in his scent, his touch, his closeness. Long ago, this had been her world for a short time.

The what-ifs of Adam being in her future could take over in seconds if she let them. But she knew, in her heart, that forever with Adam would always be only a dream. She could never live with the hurt of losing him once again.

Adam couldn't deny his nervousness as he waited for Gavin to bring his mom to the party. Surprises were already hard to pull off, and even harder when it came to Shelley Hawk.

Without Nicole there would be no party, and he couldn't wait to tell his mom about Nicole's part in taking the whole event to another level with her Christmas in July idea. Nicole coming up with this theme had really been genius. Not only did the Victorian look spectacular, but pine and peppermint scents filled the air thanks to candles.

"There's a car pulling into the driveway!" The lookout, Blair from the church, hollered, letting the curtain drop. "Everybody take their places."

Adam stood with the front line of folks hiding just inside the kitchen, across the foyer from the living room. Gavin had promised to think of a good reason to not only stop by the house, but have his grandma come inside. Everyone had decided to let them make their way into the living room before jumping out and yelling.

The door clicked open, and Adam felt his breath catch. At that moment he also wondered where Nicole had gone.

While he wanted her by his side, she had gone off to make last minute adjustments, assuring him she'd be right back.

He tried turning around, but the crowd of people prevented him from seeing anyone that wasn't directly behind him. Adam watched the backs of his mom, Kylie and Gavin head toward the living room. As they walked through the doorway the word "Surprise!" rang through the air, and Adam took the few steps to meet his mom. As she turned, the look on her face said everything he wanted his mom to feel.

"What's going on?" Shelley stepped back from hugging Adam. She focused her attention on her grandson. "Did you know about this?"

"Yes. We wanted to surprise you for your birthday. This was all Rachel, Adam and Ma's idea."

Shelley looked genuinely stunned and surprised. "Well, I'll be." Shelley looked around. "Why is everything Christmassy?"

"It's your Christmas in July party. Although you're barely sliding in on the second of the month. But, hey, it's July." Adam put his arm around his mom. "We know how much you love Christmas and if movie channels can do it, so can we. Right? There's food in the dining room, coffee in the kitchen. Everyone enjoy." The guests all clapped, and Adam stepped aside to let Shelley's friends greet her and wish her a happy birthday. He glanced around but didn't see Nicole anywhere.

Maybe he'd find her checking on the food or coffee. He mingled through the crowd, seeing everyone but her. Where could she have gone? He crossed paths with Gavin who, at this point, carried a full plate of food. Kylie followed Gavin like a shadow. "Have you seen your mom?"

"No. I wanted to sit with her, but couldn't find her."

An uneasiness spread through Adam's gut. While

there were quite a few people here, there weren't so many that someone could go missing.

Gavin set his plate on one of the tables. "I'll look for her if you want."

"I'll help find Miss Nicole, Daddy. Then we can all sit together. Like a family." Kylie slid her plate next to Gavin's.

Adam blew out a breath. *Sit together like a family?* Kylie's innocent words reminded him of the risk. Reinforced why he needed to play it cool around Nicole. "Thank you both. But, sit and eat. I'll take a look outside. She's probably chatting it up with someone." Although he wasn't sure who, since Rachel was in eye's view. Adam pushed down his fear that she might have left.

A quick look through the house and outside produced no Nicole. He even went out the front door and scanned the porch. Nothing. No one. Maybe she *did* leave? Maybe he'd been right all along. He swallowed hard at the thought.

He stepped inside and came face-to-face with his mom. She glowed with more than the sunshine she'd been basking in on her vacation, and he couldn't be happier about making her birthday special. "Are you having a good time?"

"I am. This is quite the party." Shelley grabbed Adam's hand and held it loosely. "I wanted to thank you for this surprise. And where's Nicole? I'd like to introduce Gavin to all my friends, and without Nicole, we wouldn't have this young man to introduce."

"I'm not sure, but I'll try to find her." It was worth one more look around for his mom's sake.

As he watched Shelley walk away, he looked around the party, at the decorations, at the people, and he realized what his life could be like. Partnering with someone who cared about family, who put thought and effort into making someone's special day, well, special. He shook his head. Why did these brief glimpses keep plaguing him? Nicole was leaving.

May have already left.

"Adam, you were looking for me?"

He whipped around at the sound of Nicole's voice, surprise pouring through him. "Yes. Where were you?"

She held up her phone. "I had to take a call from one of my friends at home, firming up dinner plans next weekend. Is everything okay?"

He sucked in a breath, feeling foolish that he thought she might have left the party, when in reality she was leaving his life, this town. Not new information, but important information to keep close to his heart as these family events took place. "Everything's perfect. Mom and I are ready to introduce Gavin."

When Adam and Nicole walked into the living room, Shelley stood in front of her friends, Kylie by her side. Adam nodded to his mom as he stood so close to Nicole their arms brushed.

Shelley clapped her hands. The room quieted. "Thank you all for coming to this amazing party. I now know how good all of you can keep a secret." Everyone chuckled.

"I want to thank Rachel and Adam and everyone else who had a hand in putting this bash together. I know many of you helped. And Nicole, thank you for offering your house in what I've learned was a last minute change. This is going to be a wonderful evening."

Everyone clapped among a few Amens and a couple of whistles.

"But now, I want to introduce someone very special to me. Gavin? Can you come up here?"

Adam watched Gavin sheepishly stand by his grandmother, who immediately hugged him. "This is Gavin, my grandson. A wonderful surprise and an amazing addition to the Hawk family. We're thrilled he's in our lives and I'd like everyone to make him feel welcome in Hawks Valley. As you can see, he's a young man, so I'll spare him from saying a few words."

This time silence met her words.

"Adam? Nicole? Can you come up here please?" Adam guessed his mom making this announcement, with all of her close friends and family, made Gavin's parentage official. That sounded weird, but he knew Shelley. Old school to the core, but generous at heart. He placed his hand on Nicole's back as they weaved their way to his mom.

"God works in mysterious ways. We all know that." Again silence. "His mysterious way has given this family a new grandson. Gavin has already brought so much joy into our home. Nicole, thank you. Thank you for raising such a fine son. Thank you for bringing him to Hawks Valley when you did. I may have questioned the timing when we first talked, but who am I to question God?" Her voice hitched. "We're all so incredibly blessed to have this young man in our lives. And, truly, this Christmas in July party is so appropriate. Christmas is when we celebrate receiving the best gift in the world. Jesus. Six years ago, I received a gift when Kylie was born. And just a few weeks ago, God gifted me another grandchild— Gavin. Words can't describe how happy this makes me. He might be a grown man coming into our lives, but he's a gift all the same."

There were a few Amens heard as Shelley teared up, squeezing Kylie and Gavin tight, nodding to Adam and Nicole who still stood close together. What an amazing family moment to be sure. Adam knew he needed to do everything in his power to keep this moment going for the rest of their lives. This is what family looked like.

He glanced at Nicole, her smile lighting the room, her beauty taking his breath away. A fleeting thought raced through his mind regarding Nicole becoming a part of his family, but he quickly brushed the thought aside, knowing it wouldn't happen. He needed to rejoice at this new family that God had given him.

Adam caught Gavin's eye and nodded. It was time to give Mom the photo album they'd made. "There's a gift under the tree. Gavin, Kylie, do you mind giving it to your grandmother?"

Kylie retrieved the present and handed it to Gavin, who set it on the closest table. "This is for you, Grandma."

Adam's vision blurred with unshed tears as Gavin said the word "grandma." She unwrapped the present with care, like she knew how special it was. She lifted the lid off the box and pulled out the album, a quizzical expression on her face.

Her smile couldn't have been wider as she read the words at the beginning of the book. The words written by himself, Kylie and Gavin.

"I don't know what to say." Her eyes filled with tears as she spoke. "A family album. What a precious gift."

"You've been a precious gift to us all these years, Mom. We wanted you to have something special. Every one of us helped, including Nicole."

Shelley scanned her gaze over the four of them. "What a treasure this family is. Thank you. I know this book will bring me many years of joy."

"There are blank pages at the end so we can keep adding photos and memories. A new tradition. And speaking of starting traditions, I have something for Gavin." Adam reached under the tree, pulled out a stocking, identical to the ones hanging on the fireplace, and hung it on the mantel. "For you, son. We couldn't be more thrilled than having you as a part of our family." The red stocking had *GAVIN* stitched in white across the top. Adam turned the other two stockings around, one etched with *KYLIE* and the other with *DAD*. Adam glanced at Nicole as some of the guests started moving toward the table to see the album. "God has given me an amazing family, hasn't He?"

She nodded as a tear fell down her cheek. It had to be a tear of joy.

Didn't it?

Chapter Fifteen

"**I** thought you said you had a surprise for later?" Adam asked Nicole before sipping his water as the partygoers started to dwindle. The sky darkened with the coming nightfall, and he was grateful the party had been such a hit.

"I do. Follow me."

Nicole seemed preoccupied as she led him only a short distance to the backyard. A few red cups had been left on the now deserted tables.

"It's really not that big of a deal. We hung twinkle lights."

The white lights had been strung through the trees and crisscrossed overhead, a fun party element to be sure. "This is cool. Did you do this?"

Nicole shook her head. "Nope. Gavin did all the work. He wouldn't let me on the ladder."

"Smart man."

"I directed the placement, though," she added.

Adam nodded. "I'm sure you did. It looks beautiful. Like you."

As much as he tried to push thoughts of Nicole aside, they kept invading his mind. She could still be beautiful even if she wasn't a part of his life.

Nicole turned to him. "You're just caught up in the excitement of the night. The party was a success, though, don't you think?"

"Huge success all around, thanks to you."

She shook her head. "Everyone pitched in and pulled it off."

He hugged her—a tad longer than he should have, but embracing her felt right. And when it ended, he hooked her pinky with his, unwilling to let her touch go. "You're right, but your suggestions made the night special. Personal. That unique touch that didn't come from anyone else."

She looked at him, her gaze guarded. "It went so well, I'm waiting for the proverbial other shoe to fall."

Even though she chuckled, he sensed her nervousness. If he was honest, he was nervous, too. This night did go well. A great family night to be sure. The only glitch happened when he thought Nicole had left. "What does the other shoe look like?" he dared to ask.

She lowered her gaze, her long lashes captivating him, as their pinkies slowly swung back and forth. "That Gavin would choose to live here." She looked straight at him. "And after tonight, I wouldn't blame him."

Adam swallowed hard, once again realizing his wish equaled her greatest fear. "Gavin loves you, Nicole. You and he have an incredibly strong mother- son bond. That bond will never be broken."

"Thank you for saying that. I think so, too. But I can see Gavin sliding into your family with such ease." Her deep brown eyes held the promise of unshed tears, and her lips trembled slightly.

Adam took a deep breath, shifting his gaze to the little white lights sparkling into the darkened skies. He had to admit this evening, this party, had come together perfectly. *If only—* No, he couldn't let his thoughts drift too far off. Nicole was simply passing through. She stopped here to sell her house and heal her son. Adam wouldn't make more of her short stay in Hawks Valley than it was.

They had tonight, though. He looked down at her, wondering if they could savor this moment in time. He lowered his head and his lips covered hers, softness, gentleness, sweetness and urgency crash landing in their kiss. A kiss that took him back years, yet held the promise of tomorrow. His forehead touched hers as he pulled her closer, wanting to be a part of making her world not hurt so much.

Or maybe he just wanted to be part of her world.

"Oh, we didn't mean to interrupt."

Nicole quickly stepped away from his embrace at the sound of Rachel's voice. He prayed his half smile covered up his racing heart. But then he noticed Rachel's hand held on to another, much smaller hand. The hand of his daughter, Kylie. Kylie whose smile almost reached to her widened eyes.

"Daddy!" She pulled her hand away from Rachel, then made her way down the steps as quickly as she could with her cast on, hugging his legs when she reached him. Kylie kept looking between him and Nicole, her smile never leaving.

Unsure words were caught in his throat. Adam had no idea what to say to his daughter—or Nicole. He'd need to come up with an explanation as to what she saw.

Scattered, he looked at his watch. "I didn't realize it was this late. I probably need to take Kylie home." Kylie. His daughter. The one he thought he was trying to protect.

Or was it his heart?

Nicole took another step back. "Sounds like a great idea."

"Yeah, Adam, a couple of the other ladies have done almost everything else. Gavin has taken the tables and chairs to the garage so Mr. Nelson can pick them up tomorrow morning. We've got this." Rachel couldn't contain her smile either before turning and walking inside, the door shutting softly behind her.

How would he explain that amazing kiss to anyone?

Adam glanced at Nicole, wanting desperately to say more to her.

Anticipation coursed through him as unspoken words jumbled in a chaotic mess inside his mind, but getting Kylie home took precedence. "Say good night to Miss Nicole, Kylie."

His daughter hugged Nicole's legs in what could only be described as a bear hug. "Good night, Miss Nicole."

"Good night, Kylie." Nicole's words had come out all breathy, and Adam totally understood. He had to push out his own carefully. He took Kylie's hand and they made their way up the stairs to the door.

Before he opened the door, she tugged on his arm fiercely. "Daddy?"

"Yes, princess?"

"I'm excited Miss Nicole is going to be my new mommy."

His daughter's words sliced through him. "New mommy?"

"Yes. You and mommy used to kiss like that. And I know kissing is for married people. That's what you always told me. I can't wait for Miss Nicole to marry you and be my mommy."

What had a much-wanted, not well-timed kiss done to his world? He thought about his vow to stay on a need, not want, basis with Nicole. Wants caused hurts. But if you never hurt, it's because you've never loved. Love and hurt were forever intertwined. This night revealed so many highs, that at one point he found himself almost willing to risk going through the lows again. But not at the expense of his family.

He turned to catch another glimpse of Nicole. She stood under the twinkling lights, a vision imprinted in his mind. One he didn't want to forget, yet one a little girl's false hopes wouldn't let him remember.

Nicole wasn't sure how long she lingered under the twinkling lights before deciding to go inside. All she knew for sure was that she needed to give Adam enough time to leave. She had heard multiple car doors shut and determined it was probably safe. The look on Adam's face before he went inside couldn't be forgotten, though, and she still imagined his arms around her, his kiss on her lips. But there was no doubt in her heart that there would be no more kisses. Kylie's declaration of Nicole being her new mommy rocked both her and Adam. His expression couldn't hide it.

Her heart couldn't handle it

Especially when that stocking kept flashing through her mind. That one stocking.

Not two.

She tried to convince herself that she was making too much of Adam's gesture of only adding one stocking to the mantel. He had simply been focusing on the children.

Not the parents.

Hadn't he?

Being around him made it easier to shove that bright red stocking out of her mind, but now, alone, without his words or touch near her, it stayed front and center in her brain.

One stocking was all he needed to complete his family. No amount of kisses or a child's misspoken declaration would change that.

"Nicole. There you are." Adam made his way down the steps, a combined look of pain and happiness etched across his handsome face.

"Adam. I thought you were taking Kylie home?" Nicole wasn't sure how much more of this man she could take tonight. Her pulse still raced, her lips still tingled and her heart still broke.

He nodded. "Gavin offered, of course. I wanted to let you know I explained to Kylie why you couldn't be her mommy. I mean with you leaving and all. How it wouldn't work."

Regret and sorrow cemented what Nicole already knew. "I'm sorry you had to do that. Yes, I am leaving. Going back to my home." She still hadn't told Adam that she had decided to stay for the Fourth of July celebration.

"And I did want to apologize for that kiss."

Nicole shook her head, swallowing down her hurt. "Don't be sorry. It's been building up. We had to do it. Get it out of our systems. Now it's done and over and we can move on." She tried to smile and make light of that mind-blowing kiss, but she wasn't sure how convincing she sounded. She certainly didn't convince herself.

Adam laughed. "Yeah, I guess we did. But I still won't forget it." He ran his hand through his hair. "So the closing is in the morning?"

Her gaze shifted to the Victorian, and she couldn't push away a small measure of sadness. "Yes."

"Are you ready? Everything packed? Having second thoughts?"

She crossed her arms against the night breeze. "All the above. Guilty as charged."

Adam squared his shoulders, clasping his hands together. "It was nice having you here, Nicole. And I can't thank you enough for bringing Gavin to us. Our family."

"It was time. He needs you, Adam." While those words were still hard to voice, they sounded more natural every day.

"He needs you, too. Why don't you come by the house when you're done with the closing? I got a text tonight from Saylor, the gal who is receiving the Paul Hawk Award. She opened the rescue shelter for animals. Gavin and I decided to surprise Kylie with a puppy. We ended up telling her just a few minutes ago. I thought it might take her mind off..." He hesitated a moment. "You know. Anyway, Saylor is bringing the puppy tomorrow. We'd love to have you meet the little rascal."

A puppy? No one had said anything to her. But why would they? They had their own little family, and she wasn't a part of it. Puppies and red stockings filled her mind. "I'll see."

"You won't leave without saying good-bye, will you?"

She half smiled, a slight laugh escaping. "I don't have the best track record, do I?"

He put his arm around her, and she couldn't help but meld into his side, take in his warmth, pretend like this was forever. "I wasn't even thinking about that. I told Kylie you wouldn't leave town without saying good-bye."

He hadn't asked her when she was leaving.

He hadn't asked her if she would stay.

However, he did ask her to come by tomorrow to be a bystander in an important family event. A family she would never belong to. A family she'd always be looking at through a window.

Adam kissed the top of her head. "Nicole, promise me you won't leave without saying good-bye."

His repeated whispers of that word closed the sliver

of hope this night had brought. She stepped away from his embrace, immediately feeling the loss.

The rejection.

The promise only a good-bye could bring. "I promise."

Chapter Sixteen

Nicole sat in The Corner Diner after the closing, purposefully avoiding The Morning Grind. She needed a few minutes alone, without distraction. The closing went smoothly. Joanna and Kent were thrilled and grateful and made Nicole agree to come back and visit when they were done renovating.

Another promise given.

After Adam's kiss last night, and their conversation, she couldn't sleep. Even though her heart told her just to leave, she'd run away once before, and she wouldn't do it again. The high school girl had been replaced by a grown woman. This time she'd stare rejection in the face before leaving.

A promise made secondhand to a little girl would have to be kept.

As would Nicole's own promise to herself. *Don't risk your heart again.*

She paid her bill and drove the short distance to Rachel's cute bungalow where she used her friend's spare key to enter. How like Rachel this place looked with its shabby chic decor. Nicole dragged her suitcase into the spare room and sat on the bed, the butterfly themed comforter wrinkling around her.

Why was she still so unsettled? Still so unsure?

She made her way into the kitchen and quickly found everything to make herself a cup of coffee. She looked around Rachel's living room area while the coffee brewed, spotting a devotional book on the end table. Picking it up, she flipped through pages quickly.

Deciding it couldn't hurt to take a look, Nicole grabbed her coffee and walked out to the patio. An outdoor table and chair set beckoned her to sit. She set the devotional on the table as she took in the beauty of the day. Bird feeders and birdbaths graced the back yard, along with cute wind chimes. As Rachel had mentioned, there was work to do as far as getting some grass to grow, but the place had a serene vibe to it.

A calming setting to be sure.

She, turned to the devotional for the day. She read, wondering how it could be true. *O LORD, thou hast searched me, and known me. Psalm 139:1.*

She set her coffee down and grabbed her phone. It took only moments to download a Bible app. It took longer to find the Psalm. She read all of Psalm 139, shaking her head. "Can it be true? Can God know everything about me and still love me? Accept me?" Her words came out as a whisper, carried on the slight breeze. The little garden area seemed to come to life before her eyes as her heart took in the words of the Psalm.

"I'm fearfully and wonderfully made? Me?" She read and reread the Psalm a couple of times before setting her phone on the black wrought iron table. A bird chirped and a squirrel climbed a tree as Nicole sat in awe of not only God's creation, but what He said about her.

How could she have missed that all these years? God made her, His thoughts are for her, and there was nowhere she could go where God wouldn't be.

A huge weight lifted from her. The words of God were like a healing balm as she took in every word with a new light.

Nicole had been blind to so many things, but now she clearly saw the love of God.

Free. She felt free for the first time in a long time. She didn't need to be accepted by anyone, any town, any family. God had her covered. His grace and mercy were endless and He was faithful. "Thank you, God. I'm sorry I was so stubborn and it took me so long to realize Your love for me. Please forgive me and set me on Your path. Amen."

She understood now that God knew her hurts and cares and considered them. That in itself lent a measure of joy into her hurting heart. Because yes, her heart still hurt at Adam's rejection. She'd maneuver through it, but with God this time. No more floundering on her own.

Nicole's wounded heart lifted with her new outlook on life. Her new willingness to risk her heart. Years ago she'd let unspoken words create a two-decade-long silence.

That wouldn't happen again. She wouldn't run.

Not this time.

Adam stood on his front porch and tried to call Nicole, but the call went to voice mail.

Again.

Could she still be at the closing?

Why did it feel like his world was falling apart when he thought he just managed to put it back together? He had explained that kiss, that one he couldn't forget, to Kylie. He'd come to terms with Nicole's choice to go back to Illinois. He also felt like she wouldn't leave without saying good-bye.

But what if she did?

Glancing at his watch, he calculated he had some time before Saylor brought the new puppy.

He needed advice, and fast.

He walked into his house and stopped in the living room. Gavin and Kylie were having a video game challenge while waiting on Saylor. "Hey, I have to run out for a few minutes. I'll be right back."

Gavin glanced at him, eyebrows raised. "Is everything okay?"

Adam's heart pounded. "It will be."

He drove to the airport, needing to talk to Riles about Nicole. The man was always a good sounding board with his level head and years of experience.

Had Nicole done the one thing he feared she would do? Leave? No good-byes for him, his mom, Gavin or Kylie?

Once he arrived at the hangar, he ran his fingers through his hair, relief pouring through him as he spotted Riles sitting at his puzzle table. Adam pulled out a chair and slapped his hands on his thighs. "I'm in deep trouble and need help."

Riles looked up, shifting his gaze from the puzzle to Adam. "Okay. That's an admission if I've ever heard one. What kind of trouble?"

"Nicole. I keep trying to call her, and she doesn't answer. Surely the closing is over. I think she might have left. Without saying good-bye." He took a deep breath. "Again."

"She was always planning on leaving, Hawk. What's the surprise here?"

Adam stood, shoving his hands in his pockets. "Kylie saw Nicole and I sharing a kiss after the party. Then Kylie blurted out that Nicole was going to be her new mommy, because I've always told Kylie kissing is for married people."

"Not a bad thing to tell a youngin'."

Adam nodded. "I honestly thought I saw a future with Nicole while we were kissing, but then Kylie's declaration reined me back to reality."

"Which is?"

"No future with Nicole, obviously. I mean look at her. She's already gone after one hiccup."

"*Might* be gone. And did you act like it was a hiccup or major surgery?"

Adam's heart thudded against his chest, the truth of the other man's question landing hard. "I'm just trying to protect my daughter. Trying to keep her from getting hurt. Again. Is that a crime?"

Riles scooted a puzzle piece around the table. "This piece doesn't seem to fit anywhere. Can you help me?"

Adam held his arms wide. "Man. I've poured out my heart and you want me to help you with the puzzle?"

Riles continued to study the puzzle, which was already three-fourths of the way done. "Life is like a puzzle. Some pieces fit, some don't. Like this piece, here." He held up a colorful puzzle piece. "There are several places I thought it might fit, but so far, it hasn't."

Adam stood over the table. "Are you saying Nicole doesn't fit into my life?"

"I'm not saying anything of the sort. But you can't try to jam a piece where it doesn't fit."

"You're talking in circles, man."

"Not really."

Adam grabbed the puzzle piece from Riles fingers. "This has a unique shape."

"It does. Should narrow down the possibilities. Trust me, there is a place for it somewhere in the big picture."

Adam walked over to the entrance of the hangar, taking in the blue sky, puzzle piece still in hand. "I'm honestly at a loss."

"Maybe she doesn't feel at home here? She's made a life for herself in Illinois." Riles continued to sit, but kept his focus on Adam.

"You think I should move to Illinois? Uproot Kylie from Hawks Valley?"

"Again, I'm not saying anything of the sort."

Adam stared, the looming runway. "I've made a lot of mistakes, but I'd do anything to protect my family. Kylie. She can't get hurt again."

"Isn't Kylie walking around in a cast?" Riles raised one gray eyebrow.

The puzzle piece felt heavy in his fingers. Adam turned facing his mentor. "Yes. What kind of question is that?"

"What happened to her?"

Did the old man have sudden memory issues? "You know what happened to her. She fell at her dance lesson."

"Oh, just checking. Did you arrange that lesson?"

Could Riles be any more on his nerves? "You know I did. What's your point?"

"She got hurt. Didn't she? At a dance lesson you arranged, paid for and more than likely took her to. She still got hurt."

Adam's heart rate notched up at the truth of his mentor's words. "Actually, Gavin took her, but point taken. I've been blind, haven't I?"

"You had good intentions, Hawk. But sometimes you just have to trust God."

Adam shook his head. "I keep thinking about how I can't trust Nicole. But she's human. Like me. God *is* the only One we can fully put our trust in."

Riles nodded toward the table. "You going to find where that piece goes? Or are you just going to hold it?"

Adam walked back to the puzzle, looking at the big picture. A plane flying in the air, beautiful scenery below.

But the piece he held boasted so many colors. Almost like it didn't belong, like it was packaged in the wrong puzzle.

Like he'd indicated to Nicole that Gavin had grown up in the wrong puzzle. How he missed all the milestones that his son had accomplished with her. How his life might have been better here in Hawks Valley.

Then trying to keep Kylie from becoming attached to Nicole for fear of Kylie suffering another loss. Another hurt.

He carefully studied the puzzle, seeing for the first time a family having a picnic. His piece was part of the blanket with the food. He placed the piece into the big picture. "Thanks, Riles."

"For what?"

"Having insight. I'm not sure how everything will work out, but I can't keep pushing my love for Nicole away because it might hurt me. Or anyone else. God has brought us all together again. I've been sensing Him working all around, but kept trying to control my family my way."

"You might be onto something, Hawk. Trust Him."

Adam's phone buzzed indicating that he received a text. "Riles." Adam held up his phone. "A text. From Nicole."

Riles smiled. "What's it say?"

Adam took a deep breath. "Here goes nothing." He clicked to open the text, then bit his lower lip to keep from shouting. "She wants to know if that offer to see the puppy is still on. I was wrong. She hasn't left."

Riles stood, taking a couple of steps, then patted Adam on the back. "That's good news. Just don't forget how you felt when you thought she did."

Chapter Seventeen

Adam wasn't sure if he drove home or flew home with the way his heart and mind were racing. Nicole would be over in a little while, but he had two very important people to talk with before she arrived.

He knew he would bare his heart to Nicole, but he didn't know how it would be received. But he did know there were things in life that were worth taking a risk for. Love being one of those things. How could he teach his family to take risks if he wasn't willing himself? He couldn't keep his loved ones in a bubble of only everything good happening.

Besides, how would they learn to navigate through hurt if they never experienced it? Not that he would purposely put his family in a position to experience pain, but real life consisted of many aspects.

Gavin and Kylie were sitting where he'd left them, still playing the game. "Save the game. We need to talk."

By their abrupt action of putting their controllers down, Adam guessed his voice held urgency.

"Is Saylor here?" Kylie asked, jumping off the couch, heading to peer out the front door.

"No." Adam glanced at his watch. "She's due here

in a few minutes. But we need to have a talk before she comes."

"I know," Kylie said. "I have to make sure the puppy gets food and water every day."

"No." Adam needed to reel in this conversation. "I mean, yes. But I have to talk to you about something else." Adam felt like he was in a race with Saylor's, his mom's and Nicole's arrivals.

Adam walked over and knelt down next to Kylie. He held his hands in hers. "I love you so much, princess. I want you to have a great family life, a good education. But most of all, I want to protect you from all the bad things the world has to offer. And in doing that, I found I've made a mistake."

"You have, Daddy? What kind of mistake?"

"I haven't trusted God with our lives like I should have. And all that is going to change starting now."

"Are you going to tell Ma that you love her?" Gavin asked. "Kylie told me she saw you two kissing. Besides I know all that hanging out wasn't just for my sake as you all claimed it was." He laughed and Adam joined him, standing.

Adam looked at his son, too wise for his years. "A lot of it had to do with you, but you're right. There were other topics discussed. Love grows, Gavin. Over spending time together, facing fears together."

Adam still needed to keep his promise to not make promises he couldn't keep. He looked at Kylie, specifically. "I don't know how Nicole feels about me, Kylie. I can't say she'll be in our lives in the way we want her to. But one thing I know is this—she is Gavin's mom, and she'll always be in our lives in some way. We have to meet her where that is, even if our hearts don't get what they want. I've learned I can't shelter you forever, little girl. As much as I want to, I can't. Do you understand?"

Kylie nodded. "But I know Miss Nicole will love us in her heart. She looks at you funny, Daddy."

They all laughed. Adam knew he was blessed. He had no idea how things would go with Nicole, but he knew that if he trusted God with his life, then even the mysterious things would work out. And he couldn't imagine God bringing Nicole all this way, ingraining her in Adam's life in such a way, just so that she wouldn't feel welcomed. Loved.

Loved most of all by him.

"Somebody's here!" Kylie shouted, pointing outside.

Adam walked to the front door and opened it to find his mom, a van he didn't recognize—probably Saylor—and Nicole all arriving at the same time.

Kylie rushed past him, while Gavin stayed by his side on the front porch.

"It's about to be chaos here," his son said, looking at Adam.

"It is." His heart was already in chaos. He couldn't wait to talk to Nicole. But they had to settle this puppy first.

"I'm ready." Gavin said.

"I'm not sure I am, but I have no choice." Adam started to take a step off the porch, but Gavin gently grabbed his arm.

"No. I'm ready to fly."

Adam switched his gaze from all three women exiting their vehicles to his son. "You are?"

Gavin nodded. "I am. I've missed it and I can't tell you how just being around you—no pressure, no expectations regarding me flying again—has helped me. Thank you. But don't tell Ma. I want to."

Adam wrapped his son in a hug, fighting hard to keep his tears at bay. *Thank you, God. Thank you.*

"Daddy! Look!"

"We'll continue this conversation and work out details soon," Gavin said, releasing Adam. "Let's get this chaos started."

Saylor walked toward the house, carrier in hand. Kylie followed with a bag, probably filled with supplies. His mom trailed Kylie, and a few steps behind, Nicole walked hesitantly toward the house. She looked beautiful in her yellow summer dress and sandals. He wanted to run to her, take her in his arms and tell her what she meant to him, but he knew he'd have to wait a little while.

"Isn't he cute, Daddy?"

Adam looked through the wire cage at the little golden ball of fur as Saylor came up the steps. "He sure is. Go on inside, I'll round out this crew."

Gavin held the door as Saylor, Kylie, then Shelley—whom Adam gave a hug and a kiss on the cheek, followed by a quick greeting—went inside. "Hi, Ma," Gavin said. "I'm glad you're here."

"I'm glad to be here." She gave Gavin a hug. A long hug.

When she let go, Adam took hold of Nicole's hand before she could step inside. "Hi."

"Hi. This is a bad time." She lowered her gaze.

Gavin let the storm door close, smiling at Adam.

"No. It's perfect timing, actually." He noticed she hadn't let go of his hand.

A knock on the window drew their attention away from each other. "Daddy! Come on. Saylor is letting the puppy out!" Kylie turned and ran before Adam could answer.

He would have to wait to spill his overflowing heart.

"I need to talk to you, but it looks like it will have to wait a few minutes. You're coming in, right?"

She nodded. "I have to talk to you, too. I've waited twenty-five years. A few more minutes won't hurt."

Adam breathed in deeply, remembering Who he needed to trust as he and Nicole walked into his house, hand in hand.

Within thirty minutes, Saylor had told them all about the puppy and its care. Kylie promised so many times that she would be taking care of everything, but everyone started laughing when Saylor offered to help Kylie take the dog for a walk and showed her the bag they would need when the puppy did his business, because Kylie started shaking her head and backing up.

"I'm not old enough for that." Kylie looked at Adam, then Gavin. "That's a job for the big people."

Saylor grabbed the leash. "Let me show you how to attach the leash. Then we'll all go for a walk."

Kylie nodded. In moments, they had the dog on the leash, ready to be taken out.

"Okay," Saylor said, the leash in one hand, the dreaded bag in the other. "The puppy is ready to take his walk. Who's coming?"

Kylie jumped up and down. "Me! I'm coming."

Shelley stood. "Count me out. I have to leave. There's a few things I need to get ready for the celebration tomorrow. The puppy is as cute as can be." She made her rounds giving hugs. "And let me know what you end up naming him."

Shelley walked to the front door, Saylor and Kylie following.

"I'll help you walk the dog, Punk." Gavin pulled one of Kylie's pigtails, but his gaze didn't leave Saylor.

Nicole smiled, wondering if her son was smitten by the pretty girl.

"I think the puppy has plenty of dog walkers. What do you think, Nicole?" Adam said.

She took a small breath, knowing she would be alone with him. It was time. She was ready. "Yeah, I think we'll pass this time."

"Can I hold the leash, Saylor?" Kylie asked as they walked out the door.

The storm door shut before a reply was given.

Nicole turned and locked eyes with Adam.

"Nicole, I've been trying to call you. I thought you left."

"I had my ringer turned off during the closing. I forgot to turn it back on when I left." Her breath caught in her lungs.

Her eyes misted and throat tightened.

She couldn't speak, but that didn't matter, because as much as she had to say, she didn't know where to start. "Adam." That seemed like a good place.

"Nicole. I've been wrong about so much. And I'm sorry."

She shook her head. She had to come out of this conversation with as few scars as she could. This whole family puppy drama had the power to undo everything she had resolved to do. "I've done a lot of soul-searching over the past few hours. God met me where I was, and I see so much clearer now. God knows me, made me, and I'm a part of His family. That brings joy to my heart. I don't need to strive for what I already have in God." Her heart hammered and she prayed she could speak her next words without breaking down. "Adam, you've done a great job helping Gavin heal. I know I can leave with peace in my heart. And for that, I'm thankful."

She turned slightly, blinking fast to keep her tears at bay, but immediately felt the warmth of Adam's hand on her shoulder. He pushed her hair behind her ear and she shivered at the gesture.

"You've done a great job raising our son. I can't imagine him being different in any way. He's a fine young man. I'm sorry for all the times I didn't trust that you made the right decision. There is no right or wrong choice here. You did what you thought best and look at our son now."

Nicole sucked in a breath. "But I pitted your family against my insecurities. I should have trusted that you only have Gavin's interests at heart. You're a good man as well, Adam."

He leaned in closer, leaving little room between them. "Is that all you think of me? A good man?"

"Well, you are."

"What about a good man who is in love with you? Can I be that man?"

Her heart, astonished at his declaration, wanted to float into the sky. "What?" She lifted her gaze to him.

He placed his other hand on her shoulder, running his index finger along her jaw. "I love you, Nicole. I've been playing hurt and confused, and I was for a while, but I see now why you made the choices you did. I respect them. I respect you. And I love you."

His words took root in her heart. "Is this really happening? It seems surreal. Is this real?"

"It's real. And good. And ours."

She tilted her head. "What about the stocking?"

He looked at her in confusion. "*Stocking?*"

Her mind swirled at her boldness. But she had come this far. "At the party. You hung a stocking for Gavin, proclaiming your family was complete." She bit her lower lip before taking a deep breath. "Does all this mean there will be a stocking for me on your fireplace, too?"

He closed his eyes for a moment before cupping her face. "I'm a guy who makes mistakes. I see now in trying to fully include Gavin, I hurt you. I'm sorry." He kissed her forehead. "I guess it's a good thing I have a big fireplace with a big mantle." She smiled and wrapped her arms around his waist. "As beautiful as this sounds, and as big as your fireplace might be, we *do* live in two different cities."

He tilted his head. "I hear they're always looking for pilots in Chicago."

His generous words brought her heart peace. Clarity. But she knew where she wanted to call home. "And I hear my son has a family in Hawks Valley."

His blue eyes brimmed. "Well, I just heard there's a fireplace looking for a stocking."

Complete. Full circle. Her heart's desire. Call it what you want, the moment she'd waited years for had finally arrived. "Adam, I've spoken these words in my heart so many times, but now I'm speaking them out loud. I love you."

He leaned over, capturing her lips. A kiss like no other they'd shared, because this kiss said forever.

Chapter Eighteen

Nicole sat in the front row between Shelley and Adam, waiting for the Fourth of July ceremony to start. Gavin and Kylie were on the other side of Adam, Kylie holding the leash of the new puppy. Riles sat next to Shelley.

Nicole floated in a dream.

A dream come true.

She looked around, the celebration in full force. Hawks Valley had shut down the main thoroughfare, filling it with food trucks and local vendors. All the shops on River Street were open, which was why Rachel wasn't sitting with them.

Music filled the air from a small stage not far away, while the scent of funnel cake and other delicious sweets mingled with grilled burgers, hot dogs and fried potatoes, which they had all partaken of earlier as they browsed through the shops and street vendors.

The blue sky had promised a beautiful day, and even though the temperature soared, the breeze off the river and through the valley kept everyone from being miserable. Nicole wouldn't have cared anyway. Unless they were eating or separated for some reason, her hand stayed firmly in Adam's. No way was she letting him go a second time. Not after this God-given second chance.

She had still been giddy last night when she told Rachel of her reconciliation with Adam. Rachel had been thrilled and offered for Nicole to continue her stay at her place while she navigated her move from Illinois and found a house to rent.

Her mind swirled at all the logistics, but for today, she vowed to focus on the celebration.

Being here for this all-important day did cause Nicole to reflect. She'd missed this all these years. Gavin had as well. She vowed they wouldn't be missing any more Fourth of July celebrations in Hawks Valley.

Adam pointed to the stage where the mayor fiddled with the microphone. "It's about to start."

"Are you nervous?" Nicole asked.

"Always. But once Mom and I get up there, everything seems to flow." He squeezed her hand, locking his gaze on hers. "Although seeing you sitting in the front row might distract me. So if I flub, it's on you."

"I'll be so distracted I won't notice."

They both laughed. After a brief welcome speech from the mayor, Adam escorted his mom to the stage where they presented the award to Saylor Conway, who was the youngest ever recipient of the award. As Nicole stood to clap, she glanced at Gavin who seemed to be in a daze, staring toward the stage.

Even Kylie tugging on the pocket of his shorts couldn't make him break his stare. Nicole followed his gaze to Saylor, standing next to Adam, looking gorgeous and at home. Hawks Valley was once *her* home, and now it would be again.

God knew selling the Victorian had been the right decision. Her cheeks heated as she remembered that she hadn't erased their names, written in pencil, from the kitchen bay window area. The new owners would probably repaint anyway, and it would be gone. But she and Adam weren't gone.

"I do have one more announcement to make. As you know, this award is given every year to honor my father who was killed flying in a guest to the Fourth of July celebration. It's been my family's joy to hand out this award to many amazing people over the years." Adam looked at Shelley. "It's been a privilege and an honor to share this stage together the last twenty-four years."

The crowd applauded.

"But my mom has decided it's time for her to retire her position in giving out the award. She'd like to say a few words." Adam handed the microphone to Shelley.

She waved to the crowd. "I'm not one for talking to a crowd, which is why I'm always the one handing the award to the recipient. Paul's legacy will stand strong through the years via this award, but I feel it's time for me to hand over the reins of presenting the award. My son, Adam, will of course continue in his role, but I'm turning my role over to my grandson—Adam's son—Gavin St. John."

A hushed silence hovered, but only momentarily. The thunder of applause brought immediate tears to Nicole's eyes. She watched Gavin make his way to the stage, a surprised look etched on his face as he gave his grandmother a hug, then his father.

Saylor had stepped to the side, leaving Adam, Shelley and Gavin front and center on the stage with the Paul Hawk Award backdrop behind them. Through tears and fumbling fingers, Nicole snapped a few pictures, never wanting to forget this moment.

She shoved her phone in her pocket as Kylie scooted

next to her, one little hand holding hers, while the other still held on to the puppy's leash. Kylic smiled at her and Nicole knew at that moment that this day was complete. Everything she needed was right here. Acceptance and belonging weren't things you tried to achieve or force upon others.

Rather, they were who you became when God captured your heart.

Adam escorted Shelley off the stage, then Gavin escorted Saylor, a grin Nicole had never seen before on his face. "You're beaming," Adam said, taking her free hand in his.

"I'm happy."

Gavin and Saylor walked up to their group after Saylor had fielded congratulations from people she knew. She bent down to pet the dog. "How's this little guy doing?" She looked at Kylie. "Looks like you've taken good care of him the last twenty-four hours."

Kylie blushed. "Gavin's been helping 'cause Daddy is making goo-goo eyes at Miss Nicole."

Now it was Nicole's turn to blush.

"I'm going to take Kylie and this puppy home," Shelley said. "I think we're all tired and ready to call it a night."

"Gav, will you come home, too?" Kylie asked, her hands in a praying position. "Let's play video games."

Gavin leaned down to Kylie's level. "It's been a long day, kiddo. How about tomorrow? Will that work?"

The little girl lowered her head, but instantly looked up, smiling. "Okay. I'll let you be a grown-up tonight. But tomorrow, be prepared to lose."

He stood, ruffling her hair. "Challenge accepted."

Saylor stood. "So you guys still haven't named this puppy yet? What are you waiting for?"

All eyes turned to Nicole.

Kylie moved to Nicole's side. "We asked Miss Nicole to name the puppy. But she hasn't come up with a good name yet, so we're just calling him 'Puppy.'"

Everyone laughed. Nicole's heart started beating faster at the words she was about to speak. "I think I have a name."

"Yay!" Kylie said, jumping up and down. She patted the puppy's head. "You're going to have a name, little puppy." She looked up at Nicole. "What's his name?"

"Linc."

Everyone's puzzled looks didn't surprise her. "Linc. L-I-N-C. Short for Lincoln. As in Lincoln Park, where Gavin and I made so many good memories. So Linc will be a reminder of our time in Illinois as we live our life here in Hawks Valley."

Nicole couldn't keep track of who was hugging her at what point, but when everyone stepped back, Adam's arm curled around her.

"I think it's a perfect name," he murmured.

"Me, too," Kylie said. "Let's go home, *Linc*. I love it Miss Nicole. And I'm glad you're staying."

"I am, too."

Shelley walked up and held her hands. "Welcome home, Nicole."

Nicole leaned into Adam even more as she pushed back the tears at his mom's words.

Shelley turned her attention to Kylie. "Let's get this puppy home."

"I'll walk you ladies to the car," Riles said, shaking Adam's, then Gavin's hands.

"Wait," Adam blurted. "I have something to say."

Gavin stepped in front of him. "I have something to say, first." He turned to Nicole, his smile, the one she had been waiting to see, on his face. "Ma. I'm going to fly. Adam and I are setting up a time for next week. I'm ready. And excited."

Nicole stood, stunned. She'd brought Gavin here for this very reason. For his healing. But God knew he needed so much more. They *both* needed so much more. *Thank you, God. Thank you for knowing us and for providing exactly what our hearts need.* Nicole stepped away from Adam and hugged her son. Her joy. "That's wonderful news, Gavin."

"You fly planes?" Saylor asked as Gavin and Nicole ended their hug.

Gavin nodded, looking sheepish. "Yes. If you ever need any animals flown anywhere, just give me a call."

Nicole felt like he was half kidding, but Saylor smiled and tilted her head. "Can't do that if I don't have your number."

Nicole's face broke into a grin as Adam waved his hand. "Rachel, over here."

Rachel on a break from the coffee shop, reached the group, and gave her brother-in-law a meaningful look. "Y'all. We are super busy. I can't stay long, Adam."

Nicole wasn't the only one looking confused. "Adam?"

He twirled Nicole into his arms. "I didn't plan this fully. I never imagined our scenario playing out this way. But Nicole, God gave us a second chance. Not only us, but our family. So, I have an important question to ask you."

Nicole's heart hammered as Adam got down on one knee.

Adam dug in his pocket, the feel of his mom's ring steadying him. She'd given it to him after her birthday party. Like she knew.

Moms always knew best.

He drew a long, steadying breath, knowing his family stood all around them, but he saw no one but Nicole as he pulled out the ring which represented a life full of love. A life he wanted to build with her.

With the diamond sparkling between them, Adam's gaze fixed on the woman he loved. "I had a talk with a smart young man this morning. You see, this young man had been raised by a beautiful woman. A woman who I loved and who I knew I wanted to spend my life with. So I asked this young man if I could have his mom's hand in marriage. If he would give his blessing. He said he would." Adam swallowed hard. "Like Mom said at her party, God works in mysterious ways. I won't pretend to understand everything, but I do understand one thing. I love you, Nicole. I love that you raised our son to be a strong, good man. I love that you have a passion for those you love, and that family is important to you. I want to be your family. Will you do me the honor of marrying me?"

The seconds ticked by as he lost himself in Nicole's deep, brown eyes.

Her smile betrayed her answer. "Yes, Adam. I'll marry you."

He slipped the ring on her finger. It would need to be sized down, but it fit well enough that it wouldn't fall off. "We can have our forever, Nicole. We really can."

"I finally believe that, Adam. This ring is gorgeous."

His heart swelled. "This is the ring my dad gave my mom. She wanted you to have it, Nicole. She wanted us to have it."

He watched her eyes widen. "Adam. This means so much." Her gaze momentarily shifted to Shelley. "Thank you. It's beautiful."

Adam stood, pulling Nicole into his arms. "*You* mean so much. Our forever is starting, Nicole."

"My dream has come true. God does work in mysterious ways."

He cupped her face, leaned over and kissed her. His arms slid down her shoulders, then around her waist. In moments, they were surrounded by their family, everyone congratulating them.

Kylie tugged on his hand. "Daddy. Does this mean Miss Nicole will be my mommy?"

As happy as Adam was, this aspect of life would need balance. Before he could say anything, Nicole placed her hand over his and Kylie's.

"Kylie. Your mommy will always be your mommy. She loved you very much, and that love she had for you will be with you forever. But that doesn't mean I can't love you, too. And I do." She smiled tenderly down at his daughter. "And we'll hang out and do mommy-daughter things. Things I didn't do with Gavin because he's a boy. I can't wait to watch you grow up into a young lady. One that your mommy would be proud of."

Adam's heart swelled at Nicole's words, but concern hovered as Kylie's expression seemed somewhat sad.

"But what do I call you?" Her blue eyes held a genuinely confused look.

Nicole shifted her gaze to Adam as he hesitated, not sure what to say.

"Hey, Punk. How about you just call her 'Ma,' like I do?"

Kylie burst into a big grin. "Ok, Gav. That way I'll be like you!" She jumped up and down, and Linc started trying to run.

"Hold on to that leash, Punk," Gavin said, helping Kylie with the dog.

God. Nicole looked up, knowing that He held this in His hands. Would awkward situations arise? Yes. But now she had a family that could work through things. Together.

The family antics continued as the band started playing. Adam tugged at her. "Would you like to go dance?"

Nicole nodded. "Only with you."

He held her close as everyone and everything else faded into a blur. "I'll never let you go, Nicole," he whispered in her ear.

"I wouldn't let you if you tried."

He kissed her again, excited for the day when she would be his wife. He didn't know exactly what day that would be, but it couldn't come soon enough.

Epilogue

Nicole stood in the bedroom of her childhood home five months later, looking at herself in the full-length mirror. Rachel, Shelley and Kylie all oohed and aahed at the sight of her in her wedding gown and veil.

Her white velvet dress with its lace neck, shoulders and sleeves caught Nicole's attention the minute she had seen it in Your Perfect Day, the bridal shop in town.

"You're stunning." Rachel smoothed down the veil. "We only have a few minutes. How are you holding up?"

Nicole took a deep breath. "Good. Excited and nervous, but good. I've been waiting for this day for a long time. Kylie, you look beautiful. The sweetest flower girl I've ever seen. And Shelley, your dress is so pretty, like you."

Shelley smiled. "Thank you. But you, darling, are a sight to behold. Adam is going to drop when he sees you. Now, I'm going to go be seated. Welcome to the family, Nicole. It's been a long time coming."

Shelley gave Nicole a quick hug before she left.

"Rachel, you're rocking that bridesmaid dress. Dark red really looks great on you."

Rachel smiled. "Thank you. I'm thrilled you're having

a Christmas wedding. Honestly, you couldn't have made Shelley happier. It's a beautiful night. Not too cold. It's like someone's looking out for you and your special day."

"I know," Nicole murmured. "Who would have guessed we could be married outside in December in Tennessee?"

"At the newly opened St. John Bed-and-Breakfast."

Nicole thanked God for everything regarding this day. She never imagined she'd be in her old home, marrying the love of her life.

"Ready, Ma?"

Nicole shifted her gaze to the door and gasped. Gavin looked so elegant and handsome in his black tuxedo. "You are the finest escort I've ever had."

Her son hugged her. "You look beautiful. And happy. I've never seen you look this happy."

"I am happy." She took a deep breath. "Are we ready? It's time for me to become Nicole Hawk."

Gavin gave Kylie a high five. "Punk. Look at you all dressed up. You ready to toss those rose petals?"

"Yes! I'm excited. I hope I do it right."

"You'll do great. Don't forget—Linc is going to help you." Gavin shot his little sister a wink.

Everyone exited the room and made their way down the stairs. The bed-and-breakfast had been slightly renovated and updated. Nicole and Adam's wedding was the first event to take place in the new St. John Bed-and-Breakfast.

Even though every room had been painted, Nicole couldn't pass up the chance to pull the curtain by the bay window back before she went outside. She smiled at the sight of her name and Adam's still trailing down the wall. A little bit of St. John and Hawk would remain forever together in the Victorian.

Nicole and Gavin waited at the back door until Kylie and Linc, then Rachel, made their way down the aisle, white chairs on either side. The wedding guest list was small and intimate, just like she and Adam had wanted.

When the violinist started playing the wedding march, Nicole, escorted by Gavin, walked down the aisle, Adam waiting with a smile at the flowered arch under the twinkling lights.

Gavin kissed Nicole on the cheek. "Before I take my place as best man, I'd like to say a few words."

Nicole, unaccustomed to this from Gavin, already felt her eyes tear up. Gavin wasn't a public speaker, and even though the crowd was small, this was still big for him.

"Ma. I can't tell you how happy I am seeing you happy. It means the world to me that you found the man you want to spend the rest of your life with." Gavin knelt in front of Kylie. "Hey, Punk. I'm honored to be your big brother. Just try to let me win some games sometimes, okay?"

"Maybe." Kylie smiled while everyone laughed.

Gavin stood, turning to Adam. "When you asked me if you could marry Ma, I was grateful that you wanted my blessing. It meant a lot to me that you thought enough to ask. I can't think of a better man to marry my mom. And I can't think of a better man to call 'Dad.'"

Nicole didn't care that tears fell down her face on her wedding day at this moment. Gavin and Adam hugged as Nicole noticed Adam's eyes were wet also.

Gavin took his place, standing between Adam and Riles, as Nicole handed her bouquet to Rachel. The pastor, holding his Bible, began to speak.

"Ladies and gentleman, we are gathered here today in the sight of the Lord to join these two in holy matrimony…"

The vows and the rings were exchanged as Nicole

thanked God for all the blessings He'd brought to her life. The blessings that would last not only a lifetime, but into eternity as well. After the pastor pronounced them man and wife, she and Adam exchanged their first kiss as Mr. and Mrs. Adam Hawk.

They walked side by side down the aisle, tears and smiles coming from every direction. Adam's hand held tight to hers and she knew he'd never let go.

Neither would she.

"Hello, Mrs. Hawk," Adam said as they rounded the house, away from the guests for a moment. "I'll never tire of saying that."

"And I'll never tire of hearing you say that. This day was perfect." She kissed him again, loving the feel of his arms around her, his heart forever hers.

"Lovebirds, time for pictures."

They ended their kiss, then made their way back to the arch where the ceremony had just taken place. Gavin stood to Nicole's right, Adam to her left and Kylie in front with Linc next to her as the photographer snapped photos.

"Wait." Adam turned, calling for Rachel, and whispered in her ear. As Rachel went into the house, Adam turned to the photographer. "We need one more picture when Rachel returns."

Momentarily, she came down the steps with a small bag in her hands. "Here, Adam."

Adam dug into the bag, pulling out red stockings. "Kylie." He handed her one red stocking, then gave the next one to Gavin. He left the empty bag on one of the chairs as he held three more stockings. "Linc? Here's yours."

Laughter rang out as Adam tried to hook the stocking on Linc's collar, which didn't work, so he handed Kylie the stocking. "Here you hold it."

After pulling another stocking out, Adam handed it to Nicole. "Mrs. Hawk, here is your very own stocking."

As if she hadn't already shed enough tears, seeing the white stitching of the word *MA* on the stocking caused more. "This is beautiful."

"Everybody, hold your stockings up. After all, this is a Christmas wedding."

Nicole glanced sideways as they all held their stockings. Everyone smiled and there couldn't be a more perfect ending to this day.

They were a family. A family knit and held together by God's love. And as surprised as she was at this beautiful second chance, she knew none of this surprised God.

And for that, she would be forever thankful.

* * * * *

Dear Reader,

I love a good reunion romance and had fun with the idea of a couple reuniting after twenty-five years. Add in an adult son and a six-year-old daughter, and what could go wrong? Just about everything, right?

Welcome to Hawks Valley, nestled in the Tennessee Valley, where Nicole and Adam navigate their way through hurt, betrayal and secrets. I pray I did the story line justice on the journey to the fall-in-love ending I so love to read about. Escaping into a story is one of my favorite pastimes, so what a thrill to have the privilege of writing a story for the Love Inspired line, whose stories about love, hope and redemption, all found through God, are inspiring.

Thank you for reading Nicole and Adam's story. I love connecting with readers. You can find me at my website, lindipeterson.com. From there, you can find my links to Facebook, Instagram and Twitter.

Lindi Peterson

HARLEQUIN PLUS

Try the best multimedia subscription service for romance readers like you!

Read, Watch and Play.

Experience the easiest way to get the romance content you crave.

Start your **FREE TRIAL** at
<u>www.harlequinplus.com/freetrial</u>.